Deadly Pawn

W. M. Stahl

For My Seventh or Eighth Grade English Teacher
For giving me the desire to write,
If I could only remember her name.

About the Author:

W. M. Stahl was born and raised in a small village in central New York. Has traveled extensively throughout the U.S. and is now residing somewhere could be anywhere, but wherever he is, he isn't there. And he can prove it.

"Having been from here to there and back again I can safely say that I all I really need is a library full of books, and an endless supply pens, paper, and cocktails." W. M. Stahl

He tipped his hat back on his head and stuffed a cigarette between his lips. The rain had almost stopped, but the damage was done and the paper streamers lay in ruins about the street. It was to have been a homecoming celebration for one of the boys from the neighborhood. As well thought out and planned as it was it seems that Mother Nature had another idea.

"Too bad about the rain," she called from across the street.

"Yeah, it is," he returned striking a match and lighting his cigarette.

They were the only two on the street so he knew that she had meant it for him.

She was a cute brunette named Carolyn but she told everyone her name was Sally, why she chose to go by that name was a secret she kept to herself. Her eyes matched her hair and her face was thin and long like the rest of her.

Her hands were worn and looked a bit frail for a woman as young as she was. Maybe it was just because she was so thin but her long fingers gave her hands the look of a woman much older than her twenty four years of age. Like the hands of an old laundress he once knew all cracked dry and rough. As if she had soaked them in lye every day from the age of five. He was sure she was a beautiful girl growing up. Perhaps even before what had happened that made her change her name and move into the neighborhood from wherever it was she'd been living before.

It's a big city it's easy to hideout from your past. Even your present if you know where to go and what to do. Changing neighborhoods and your name is a good way to start. He'd only figured out who she was a few months earlier after seeing her in one of the bars uptown. An old client had asked him to see if he could find her, but without any idea of the girls past he didn't have many places to start. There wasn't much for him to go on, the chances of finding her were thinner than a thin dime and he'd told him so. All he had to go on besides her name and a bad photograph was the name of the speakeasy they'd met in a couple of years earlier. Poppies Showroom had been the name of it, now it was somebody's basement apartment.

She'd been sitting alone in one of the booths of a nightclub he'd stumbled into when he spotted her. She was likeable girl, easy enough to look at so he gave a polite salute with his hat as he sat down at the bar. He did however notice the panic in her eyes as soon as she noticed him, so he stayed away letting her breathe a little easier. Still she kept one eye on him for the entire time he was there. Everyone seemed to know her as a long line of customers all said hello as they happened to slip past her booth.

It would have been hard for him to miss them all calling her Sally and he couldn't help but notice her look at him each time they did. Those few months earlier and the thin looking woman hadn't looked so frail. The name and the face didn't connect until he'd sobered up the next day. It didn't take him long after that to figure out that Sally was Carolyn Walsh, linked to one of societies best known names in the city. Luckily for her none of the people in the neighborhood she lived in now read the society pages a fact, he believed, she was counting on. If any of them read anything beyond the sports pages or racing forms would be news to him. Even if they did, it had been a couple of years ago and a neighborhood like this one has a short memory. He made the call to his old client and left it at that.

The street was empty now except for him. The rain had returned and he pushed himself deeper into the front window of the barbershop. An overhang for the marquee helped to keep him dry for the most part. Stubbing out his cigarette on the sidewalk with his foot he began to wonder if he wasn't being stood up. The note had said for him to meet them there, in front of the barbershop. It also said that they would be there at seven; it was nearly eight by the clock on the wall inside. He stuck another cigarette between his lips and was about to light a match when a black sedan pulled round the corner at the opposite end of the street. It moved slowly toward him making him question if this was who he'd been waiting for. Tossing the unlit cigarette to the ground and stepping around the edge of the building, he reached into his jacket wrapping his hands tightly around the butt ends of his twin forty-five Colt automatics.

As the car got closer he watched through the rain as the muzzle of a Chicago typewriter pushed its way out of the passenger side window. It was then he began to think that the note had only intended to get him there for this. As the first passenger leaned out of the window another one followed from the back seat. The car slowed as the guns barked and a hail of bullets tore into the shop windows beginning a few doors before the barbershop. The guns blazed on until they rattled to a halt when each of the guns clicked empty. A few stray bullets hit the corner of the alleyway and barbershop wall before they ricocheted harmlessly away. Dawson found himself down on one knee in the pouring rain as the sedan sped off down the street and around the corner several blocks away. Still gripping his twin forty-fives, he wasn't sure why he wasn't firing back. Shaking his head he muttered to himself as he stood up.

"Not today ladies," he said aloud as he shoved them back into his shoulder holsters.

Mob shootings weren't really any of his business. Sure there may have been an occasion or four when one or three different mobs may have tried to kill him in the past. Then again he wasn't supposed to even be back in town yet so it was unlikely that they had been meant for him. He shook the thought out of his head knowing there was little chance that they had even seen him standing in the shadows. Still there hadn't been anyone else on the street they could have hit, except for him. Just the same he took a few seconds to take another look on the off chance that he'd missed something or someone and they'd been hit. Other than a few broken windows that would now let the rain into the effected shops, everything looked the same. If they had meant to hit him they would try again, and next time he would let his ladies bark back.

The rain ran from the brim of his hat in a steady stream and he was pretty sure as he stood there it was going to be running down the back of his neck off his shirt collar soon. So much for my dry cleaning bill this month, he thought. Pulling out a cigarette he cautiously looked up the street checking once again that it was all clear. He paused as he went to strike the match to light his cigarette as if he were waiting for the car to appear again. Satisfied they wouldn't be coming back around the corner, at least not any time soon, he finally struck the match and lit the snipe a second later. It was then that he heard Sally scream.

"They shot him," she sobbed. "Those dirty rotten …"

She turned as he came through the door of the little pawnshop, staring at him with tears streaming from her big brown eyes. He could tell that she wanted to throw herself at him as she took a half step before looking back at the old man on the floor. Most of the kids in the neighborhood called him Pop or Mr. Morre. He liked to call him Mack.

"Awe Mack," he said; his cigarette dangly from his lips. "Why would anyone want to put a slug in you?"

Kneeling down he placed a hand on Mack's chest. He wasn't sure so he waited a second longer before saying anything. The chest rose slightly and Mack opened his eyes briefly struggling with the pain. He ripped off his overcoat and rolling it into a ball placing it gently behind his head.

"Don't just stand there," he shouted, "get the police, get an ambulance do something."

But she was already gone and there was no one there to hear him. Pulling a few shirts from a shelf nearby he pushed them into the holes in Mack's body. The old man reached up and took hold of his arm. Lowering his head he could feel the old man's breathing becoming shallow as he continued to struggle to breathe.

"That's it pal hang in there," he said tossing his cigarette toward the door.

Pop opened his eyes again staring up at him. Struggling to breathe he pulled him closer and began to whisper in his ear.

"What's going on here?" Officer Riley yelled as he came through the door.

"What do you think is happening?" Dawson asked looking up at him.

Riley turned and called back outside out for an ambulance. Down the street Rookie Officer Carl Benson had opened the callbox and was already talking to the station.

"Yeah, that's right," he repeated into the call box receiver, "the pawnshop on Thirty-Eighth and hurry."

He didn't wait for an answer as he hung up and ran to the shop.

"Well Dawson, as always it looks like you have a little explaining to do," Riley said as he looked down at him.

Officer Jason Riley was a flatfoot, a beat cop. The one all the jokes were about and every stereotypical beat cop ever made before or after owed it to Riley for the definition. He knew everyone on the street and none of them thought much of his skills as a cop. If you needed to know where the truants were hiding out or who was stepping out on whom then Riley was your man. However, if you needed to solve a crime Riley was the last man you looked for. He was also the last cop anyone would think was on the take, everyone was sure he wasn't smart enough to worry about catching on to anything.

Officer Carl Benson had been working with Riley for little over a month. Some gave little hope for him being any better than Riley. Then again he was new on the beat and no one knew for sure what kind of a cop he was going to turn out to be.

Dawson shook his head and hoped that Riley wasn't the only

cop on duty in the precinct. He wasn't overly excited as the rookie walked in behind Riley. Paying little attention to Riley, Dawson worked instead on stopping the bleeding from the old man's body. He was relieved as the rookie cop knelt on the other side of the pawnbroker offing his assistance, but not for long.

"Never mind that Benson," Riley scolded, "that's not your job. Get outside and keep everyone out of here."

The rookie didn't say a word. The look in his eyes said it all as he rose slowly and went back out into the rain.

"So why'd you shoot him?" Riley asked for the third time in as many seconds. "Let's have a look at your heater; I know you have one Dawson hand it over."

Dawson looked out of the corner of his eye at Riley. It wasn't as if he was hiding them. Everyone that knew him knew that he was never without his 'girl's.

"I don't suppose you have a permit for those," Riley cracked trying to sound important.

"Come on Riley you know better than that," Dawson returned more than a little put off by the question. "We've been through this before. I guess you haven't eaten yet. Craving a little crow dinner are you?"

Riley didn't like Dawson and it showed, but then there was little in the neighborhood that he did like. Showing his contempt for the man he asked once more to see his carry permit.

"Signed sealed and delivered by the Mayor himself," Dawson said as he handed the card to the officer before turning back to the injured man.

Outside Officer Benson was looking at the damage done by the Thompsons. The shattered windows and pock marked walls that began at the bookshop, the business before Pops pawnshop, across the dress maker on the other side and didn't stop until the barber shop and the alleyway just beyond it.

Soon the street was filled with on lookers huddled around the door of the pawnshop, each holding an umbrella against the rain. Each that is except Sally who stood next to the door between the bookshop and the pawnshop. The alcove made by the entryway to the upstairs offered little protection from the rain. Her hair was matted to the sides of her face and her thin overcoat was soaked through. It did however hide the tears that continued to flow from her eyes. Until slowly, she pushed unnoticed out from the ever increasing crowd and disappeared into the night.

As the sedan rolled around the corner the three men inside were discussing their handy work.

"That should send the message that the boss ain't messin around with these people."

"I hope so," the driver added checking his mirror for the third time to see if they were being followed yet.

"What do you think Two Time?" the first of the three asked.

Two Time sat in the back seat drying the rain off his Thompson and staring straight ahead.

"We gotta go back," he shouted sitting on the edge of his seat. "I seen her, we gotta go back."

"We ain't goin back there now Two Time," the driver added. "The place will be crawlin with cops by the time we get back there."

"Who'd you see," Stitch; the first one asked.

"That skirt da boss been lookin for."

"Aw go on that dame ain't in a thousand miles of here or we'd ah known it by now."

"Yeah she's been gone almost a year," the driver; Shifty added.

Joe 'Shifty' Barton, Carlos 'Stitch' Carlotti, and Eddie 'Two Time' Haggerty all grew up together in the same poor neighborhood on the east side. Each a product of their environment and none of them looked anywhere but at themselves for what they turned out to be, muscle and trigger men for hire. The three men talked about whether or not they should tell their boss as they drove out to the small nightclub and motor cabins in the country where they were supposed to have been all night, that is according to their alibi.

Minutes pass like hours when you're waiting for help and it seemed like hours before the ambulance pulled up to the curb. The crowd, as they always seem to do, parted allowing the doors to open and the people inside of it to do their job.

"Dawson," cried the plain clothed detective as he walked into the pawnshop behind the ambulance doctor and driver. "I should've known. What are you doing here I thought you were supposed to be out of town?"

"Me," Dawson said with a slight smile for his old friend, "I was invited of course. I thought you were on special assignment with the governor?"

"Eh, turns out we don't like each other much," he returned. "I want to put an end to organized crime while he just wants to take their money."

"That would do it I suppose."

"So tell me Riley do you have the man in custody that committed the crime yet?"

"I do Abrams, I do," Riley said pointing at Dawson and handing the detective his forty-fives.

"Now that is some trick Riley," Abrams said smelling the ends of their barrels. "These were able to put all the holes in the buildings outside and into the old man without smelling like they were fired recently."

"I suspect he thinks that I cleaned it before he got here," Dawson smiled knowing that it wouldn't help his case with Riley. "Stuffed them back in my holster then knelt down to help Mack. Then again maybe I cleaned them right in front of him after he got here."

Riley again gave Dawson his best look of contempt to which Dawson merely smiled one of his own. Abrams pulled Riley outside before the officer forgot that he was on duty and took a swing at Dawson.

"You need to lay off him a little," Abrams said when he returned. "We all know he's a lousy cop, still you don't need to prove it to him every time you see him."

"You know me Chester," Dawson replied pushing his elbow into his old friend.

"That's the trouble I know you too well," he returned.

"I'm just trying to do for the city what they can't seem to do for themselves."

"I'm afraid to ask what that is," he chuckled.

"I'll tell you if you insist."

"No, for heaven's sake don't," he continued, laughing now. "How about you just stick to telling my how it is that you happen to be here."

"Like I said Chester I was invited," Dawson handed him the note that he had stuffed in his pocket earlier in the evening.

With the note in his right hand he took his left and reached for his pack of cigarettes in the breast pocket of his shirt. The movement was smooth, as if the two hands had practiced that same movement a hundred times a day.

Lighting his cigarette he told Abrams what had happened as he saw it. He left out seeing Sally thinking it would be in her best interest to not involve her, at least until he had a chance to talk to her. He also neglected to tell him that the pawnbroker had talked before Riley stumbled in.

"What are you going to do now?" Abrams asked when he finished.

"Me," Dawson replied as he watched the doctor and his driver carry their patient out and load him in the ambulance. "I'm going around the corner to Mike's Place for a cocktail, this one's all yours. I got no dog in this chase."

"You're not even curious to find out who sent you that note?"

"The only thing I'm curious about right now is why I don't have a cocktail in my hands. Besides I think I already know who sent it."

With that Dawson tipped his hat and walked out of the pawnshop. Pausing to watch the ambulance pull away from the curb, he was surrounded by reporters.

"What do you know Dawson?" two of the more eager types asked even before he was completely out the door.

"I know lots of things," he began as he pushed his way through them. "For instance, I know that you gentlemen are keeping me from a cocktail."

"What's so unusual about that," returned one of the reporters in the group before laughing.

His laugh infected all of them making Dawson raise his hand to quiet them.

"Good point Tiny," he added recognizing the voice. "But I can't tell you a thing."

He paused for effect then looked around to make sure he had them all hanging on his words.

"I'm strictly a bystander in this one boy's and you can all quote me if you want to," he said finally pointing his finger toward the sky and giving it a little wag. "This one is all Abrams' baby so you're going to have to talk to him about it."

"Aren't you a lot of help," Abrams said stepping out behind him.

"Do you know who did this?" one of them asked immediately.

"Do you really have to ask that," he returned looking disgusted with them already. "You guys can draw whatever conclusions you want and I'll let you. All I want from you in return is that you keep any mention of this guy they call Pop out of it. If I find even the mention of his name out side of the fact that he owns the store I'll personally put the cuffs on you, got it?"

"Yeah we get it Abrams," Tiny spoke up for the group, "but you owe us one."

"I owe you one?" he laughed. "You guys have pretty short memories if you think I'm going to owe you one."

"Okay, okay," one of the other reporters added. "Just know that this one comes off of your side of the column.

"I had no doubt that it wouldn't," he began again. "Look fellas we all know who's behind this and quite possibly why. I don't think we need to panic the rest of the business owners in the city just yet. I don't want anyone of them to know that anything was hit besides the buildings."

"Whatever you say Chester," Tiny returned, "right guys?"

"Yeah sure no problem," almost all of them said in unison.

"You sure they'll stick to that?" Dawson asked as they walked away from them.

"They better," he returned, "on second thought maybe I should look n' see if know where my cuffs are."

"That shouldn't be too hard Chester, all you have to do is remember where you were the last time you and the misses played cops and robbers."

"Dawson!"

Sally had slipped away from the crowd easily, maybe too easily, but she couldn't stand there any longer someone was bound to notice her. She wasn't as worried about Dawson remembering her as she was about the reporters and cops. If they found out that she was there or anywhere near there when it happened they'd be back, she was sure of that. When they did, Pop wouldn't be the only dead person in the neighborhood.

When she felt she was far enough away she ducked into a coffee shop and went straight for the phone booth. Digging into her bag she found the number that was written on a used matchbook. It was crumpled from having been thrown away more than once. Although she always found herself digging it back out of the trash minutes later. Finding some change she dropped it into the phone. Hearing the words 'number please' she asked the operator for the number. As she hung her bag back over her shoulder the butt end of her thirty-eight revolver caught on the opening hanging halfway out of it.

"It's me Carolyn," she said when her party answered. "I need your help."

As she listened she looked nervously out the windows of the booth. Spotting the waiter cleaning up she looked away and lowered head hoping that he hadn't gotten a good look at her. Dropping her hand to her side she felt the gun butt hanging on the cloth lip of the bag. Her eyes went wide as she stuffed it back in and looked back at the still busy waiter. Hoping that he didn't see the gun she tried to calm herself. What could he do anyway she wasn't the only girl in town that carried a gun. Although she was sure that she was the only soaking wet person in that diner that was carrying a gun. Her being soaked would make anyone wonder what she was up to, seeing her gun would have made them suspicious on top of it.

"I'm not sure," she returned finally. "Wait let me ask."

"What's the name of this place?" she asked sticking her head out of the booth.

"Liberty Diner," the waiter answered without looking up.

She thanked him before repeating it into the phone. She waited for an answer again while watching the waiter wipe the counter. She was surprised that there was no one there but then again it was early and maybe most of their trade was later or perhaps even earlier.

"Yeah, I can do that," she answered into the phone, "please hurry."

She hung up the phone and gave an audible sigh of relief and looked about the diner for a place to sit where she couldn't be noticed easily.

Stepping out she found a small table half hidden by the phone booth itself.

"Little girl's room," she asked.

The waiter finally looked up and pointed around the end of the counter where she was standing. He smiled when he saw her and wanted to comment on the rain, but didn't think that she needed to be reminded about it. Grabbing a cup and saucer he set it on the end of the counter and filled it with coffee. Pulling a nickel out of his pocket he paid for it himself just in case she didn't have any money left.

In the ladies room she tried to dry herself out as best as she could. Trying not to think any more about what had happened instead she focused only on what she needed to do right then. All she had to do now was dry off a bit and sit tight until he came for her. Then her nightmare would be over and soon behind her. She wasn't sure that turning to him for help was the best idea, but it was better than some of the alternatives. Sure he wasn't the only one she could turn to for help, but he was the only one she felt she could trust.

So okay, she thought, trying to satisfy her reasons for calling him. When he'd given her the number he hadn't meant for her to use it when she was in trouble. He'd meant that she should use it in case she wanted to see him or if she needed anything. Not when she was afraid for her life, running and hiding from people that might want her dead. Then again a way she did need something, she needed to get away, she needed to hide, and she needed help.

When she was satisfied that she had done all that she could to dry off she ventured back out into the diner and made her way to the booth she had found. He noticed her as she came out; she looked a little better but still looked pretty wet.

"If you want I can put your coat back in the kitchen next to the grill," he said setting the cup of coffee in front of her. "It'll dry pretty fast back there."

She shook her head and thanked him for the coffee and dug back into her bag to pay for it.

"Don't bother," he said, "I already paid for it. I wasn't sure if you had any money after your phone call and well I figured it was the least I could do. You hungry?"

"Soup and half a sandwich?" she asked more than stated.

"Sure no problem," he returned "I'll be right back."

Don't hurry she thought, on the off chance that they had seen her go into the diner she wasn't in any hurry to get any more innocent people hurt tonight.

"I forgot to ask you want kind of sandwich you wanted," he said sticking his head back out of the kitchen.

"Whatever you have your hands on will do fine," She replied.

She wasn't hungry but the hot soup sounded good. Along with the coffee it should do the trick in warming her up.

"Are you sure I can't hang your coat up in the kitchen," he said Placing the soup in front of her. "It'll dry quick back there I promise."

She shook her head again.

Taking off his starched white cap he sat in the booth across from her. She didn't protest but wasn't very happy just the same. He would want to talk to her and she wasn't in much of a mood to talk at least not about what he wanted to.

"You from around here," he asked.

"How come you're here by yourself?" she asked in return trying to get him off the subject of her.

"Cooks in the back," he said gesturing to the kitchen. "He don't come out here much."

"No I mean how come there isn't anyone here, you know customers."

"Oh, we pretty much only have walking trade here. When it rains we get nobody for hours on end. Once the clubs close the place packs up for a few hours no matter what it's doing outside."

She wasn't really listening as she sipped at the soup and took a couple bites from the sandwich.

"Are you ready," called a voice from the door.

She looked up to see him standing in the door. Taking up nearly the entire opening, his shoulders were just inches from touching either side. He wore a long black overcoat and a black hat that dripped a little rain as he waited.

"How much does she owe you," he asked.

His deep voice echoed through the empty diner.

"Uh, um, fifteen cents," he said half gulping at the sight of him.

"Thanks again," she said quickly producing two bits and placed it gently in his hand.

She had a hard time keeping herself from smiling as she noticed how scared the young waiter seemed to be as the big man spoke. Standing up she practically ran to him. Taking his proffered arm he quickly hustled her out of the diner and into the waiting car. It was warm and dry, and she settled quickly in the back as he jumped into the driver's seat. The time might come she thought, as they drove quickly away, when she would have nowhere to turn and be out in the cold for good, but not today.

An hour and a half later she was in a hot bath sipping brandy and smelling nothing but lilacs and roses. She didn't realize how much she had missed the world of brandy and hot baths until now. She would be safe there, for a while anyway. Just how long she would be safe remained to be seen. Until then she was sure she would enjoy her time there. It might be hard to take, she chuckled at the thought of it, but she was sure she would be able to work it out. Yes, she thought, having him help her could be quite enjoyable if she could work it out. Yet as hard as she tried she couldn't help but see Pop lying dead on the floor of his shop. She knew that they might want to kill her, but she didn't think they would resort to turning the street into a shooting gallery to do it.

"I'm sorry Pop," she cried softly and sank below the water.

"Erythin aw-rite in dere Miss Carolyn," the maid called from behind the door a few minutes later.

"Heavenly," Sally sighed taking another sip of her brandy.

"Why you jus holler or push on da button when you be ready and I come runnin," the girl called back before going back to picking up Sally's wet clothes.

"Sure gonna be good havin Miss Carolyn here again," added a second maid as she set a pile of clean dry clothes on the bed.

"Uh hmmm," the first maid, Jamie, nodded her head as she spoke. "Why, the mister he be a smilin ah ready."

"He a whole lot easier to take whenever Miss Carolyn be here that's for sure," added the second.

The two giggled as they finished up and left the room.

Passing the 'Mister' in the hallway they let him know that she was safely in the bathtub and that they were taking care of her.

"Very good," he returned. "Oh, and Jamie, you can't tell anyone that she's here."

"Not even momma?"

"Not even your mother, understand."

"Yes sir I understand, I won't be tellin no one. You can count on both uh us." Jamie answered nodding toward the other maid.

The second maid nodded as well, affirming her cooperation. He smiled and pressed a hand on each of the girl's shoulders before turning away and going to stand for a moment in front of the bedroom door. Satisfied that the two maids would take care of all her needs for now, he went to his own room to change. There was a lot that needed to be done between then and the time she finished her bath and he didn't want to waste any more time. When he finished changing he picked up the phone and dialed the carriage house letting it ring twice before hanging up. His chauffeur didn't need to answer, the two rings told him when and where he needed to meet his boss. When he was ready he came out of the side door next to his private office carrying two sandwiches and a medium sized box. He handed the big man the box before getting into the back seat.

"Remind me to thank Cook for this," he told his boss as he settled in.

"I'm sure that she will be the one reminding you when she knocks on your door for payment," he told him with a wink. "Just be careful she doesn't wanna make an honest man out of you any time soon."

It was hard to see it in the darkness of the car but the big man blushed at the knowledge that his boss knew anything about him and the cook.

Mike's Place wasn't much to write home about. It definitely was a long way from the nightclubs that one might see in the movies. They did have a piano on a little stage in the back and a place marked out on the floor where customers, if any wanted to, could dance. Dawson never went anywhere to dance.

"You're late," Jane called to him from the bar.

He shook his head as he checked his hat and coat. He apologized to the buxom blonde behind the counter for their being so wet.

"That's ok Dawson," she said recognizing him "I'll put them close so I can dry them for you."

Smiling he winked at the girl as he reached out to touched her chin.

"That's right honey," he added, "you just stand real close to them and they'll be dry in no time."

Batting her eyes at him she smiled showing off her best dimples.

"Come on lover boy," Jane said dragging him away from the hat check room. "I swear if I didn't keep my eye on you there would be no telling where you would be by morning."

"I am quite sure where ever I was I would be in very good hands," he added looking over his shoulder giving the blonde another wink as he was led away.

"Honestly Dawson I think you do this on purpose, leaving me all alone here. Making me jealous and keeping me waiting for you for hours."

Jane had little to worry about, there was little chance that she would be alone long if she didn't want to be. She stood a little over five foot six and her long raven colored hair outlined her milky complexion perfectly. She had curves in all the right places and enough of them to cause a few car wrecks when shown properly. Baby blue eyes under her dark bangs finished the picture.

Benny, the manager, spotted him as she was dragging him toward the bar.

"Dawson," Benny called as he came closer. "Follow me I have your table for you."

Dawson shrugged his shoulders and followed obediently with Jane in tow.

Benny pointed to a table near the stage that had a couple already sitting at it. Two waiters were there immediately chasing the couple away. The man knew better than to argue about it.

Although the girl with him wasn't as well informed until he whispered in her ear. Noticing them being chased away Dawson tossed his hands in the air as if to apologize when they looked his way.

"I really wish you would call ahead," Benny added as he

seated them. "I would have gotten the chef to prepare something special for you."

"Never fear Benny" Dawson said as he sat down. "Whatever he makes will do just fine."

The couple the waiters had chased away were being given another table closer to the bar. One that was more crowded for sure but Dawson was happy that at least they weren't being tossed out.

"I hope that you're going to buy their drinks."

"Whose drinks," Benny laughed. "You know I only buy drinks for you"

"Are you telling me that you're going buy the drinks for my table tonight?"

"Of course," Benny said a little condescending, but knew that if his boss ever found out that Dawson was there and he didn't buy him drinks he would be without a job. "I am always happy to buy your drinks."

He touched Jane's shoulder as he finished and nodded his head giving her his best 'you betcha' wink.

"Good," Dawson smiled back at him as he stood up and walked over to the young couple.

"What's he doing now?"

"How should I know I am just his date," Jane giggled.

Borrowing an empty chair he sat and talked to the young couple. They were surprised by the visit and as Dawson talked they both tilted their heads as if they were trying to hear him better. Grabbing one of the waiters as he passed Dawson pointed to his table and back to the young couple. Nodding his head the waiter understood what he was being told then disappeared into the kitchen. Standing up he found his way back to Jane after waving to a few of the other guests as they called out his name. As Jimmy the piano player was coming back from his break he waved Dawson over to him.

"Hello Jimmy," Dawson said taking his hand. "It has been a long time."

"Too long I think."

"What's on your mind?" he asked him.

He'd known him long enough that he didn't usually take time out from his playing unless there was something he wanted to know. Everything else would generally wait until he went on another break.

"I just heard about what happened," Jimmy looked around the room quickly as he talked. "You think Pop is going to make it?"

"I wouldn't want to say for sure, but the doctor was hopeful."

"Got any ideas yet?" Jimmy couldn't help himself from continually checking the room; something that didn't escape Dawson's notice. "You know they went to see him yesterday don't you?"

"Why, no I didn't know that." He could only guess who Jimmy was talking about, but he knew better than to let on, at least for now.

"Yeah, you think maybe things didn't go so well?"

It was his turn to tilt his head slightly and nod as if he knew what he was telling him.

"I better get back to work before Benny catches me," Jimmy shook his hand again. "You need to come in more often we've got a new singer that's right up your alley."

"Oh really," Dawson glanced toward Jane before smiling and raising his eyebrow. "In that case I better stay long enough for the floor show."

Jimmy took his seat at the piano with scattered applause to welcome him back.

Finally taking his seat Dawson tossed his pack of cigarettes on the table and smiled at Jane.

"I hope you missed me terribly," he said hoping to at least make her smile at him.

"You know I always miss you," she returned. "I'm just not so sure how terrible it is."

Dawson raised his eyebrows and groaned at her joke.

"You'd think we were in the Sahara and not a bar." He quipped as he looked around several seconds before finding their waiter. "Ah, finally; did you get everything taken care of?"

"Of course," he replied as he came to the table.

"Very good, I think we'll start with a couple manhattans then."

"Right away," the waiter replied and turned to leave.

"Oh you better make that three, one for the little lady over there."

"At least you didn't forget me this time."

"You know if I ever forget you it's simply an over sight and nothing more."

Smiling the waiter turned and waved three fingers in the air toward the bartender as he walked away.

"I think they know you too well here," Jane mused.

"Either that or I have become too predictable in my old age."

"Old age," Jane began, "why you're not a day over ..."

"Eh, tut, tut my dear mustn't say such things, at least not out loud."

"Yes, heaven forbid one of these twenty two year olds hear how old you are, they'll be running for the hills."

"Actually I am more worried that they might want me to be their Daddy." Dawson chuckled in spite of himself. "You're not going to be jealous again are you dear? You know it doesn't do you well."

"You never once told me that I was anything more than a date so I can't be sure how I would ever have a chance to be jealous."

"You see that's why I like you so much. Never once do you want to scratch out the eyes of the competition. That makes my life so much easier knowing that I never have to argue with a woman about other women."

"If you say so dear," Jane returned with a wry smile.

As soon as the waiter set her drink in front of her she slugged it back and asked for another.

"You better hurry up dear," she called as she reached for his second drink. "You're falling behind already."

Dawson laughed and held up four fingers for the hovering

waiter.

With Jimmy playing on his piano there were a few couples that were up dancing though not many. When they finished with their dance the young couple headed toward Dawson and Jane's table and as if on cue waiters brought over two chairs.

"Thank you for inviting us over Mr. Dawson but I think that we really shouldn't …" the young man began.

"Nonsense," he returned, "Benny shooed you away from a great table and wasn't even going to compensate you for it. He is paying for our drinks so if you sit here he pays for yours as well."

"Certainly Mr. Dawson but we can't impose on you honestly."

"You certainly had better impose Mr. … Mr. …" Jane began.

"Roberts, James Roberts," the young man began, "and this is my wife Ann."

"Pleasure to meet you both," Jane said pushing her hand toward the young woman. "You'll have to forgive him he seems to have other things on his mind."

Dawson was waving for the waiter again as he eyed the curvaceous long haired brunette sitting on the piano bench next to Jimmy.

"Yes sit," Dawson said as if he were brought back to reality. "Jane this is James and Ann they were married last week. You could say they are on their honeymoon tonight."

"Then I insist that you sit with us," Jane added kicking at Dawson under the table. "I think it'll do him some good to rub elbows with a married couple, maybe something with rub off on him."

"Hey, let's not go that far," Dawson laughed as the couple finally sat down. "You know how I feel about that subject."

"Yes dear I know," she said before quoting him. "A husband is what's left of a sweetheart after his nerve has been killed."

"Exactly," he said laughing, "and you know I'm not quite ready to have my nerve killed."

They all laughed as the waiter brought them a round of drinks.

"Dawson," Jane added after a few seconds.

"Oh, don't worry," he said waving a hand at her. "His nerve was ready to be killed."

Nodding his head toward the young groom he smiled waiting for what he knew Jane would say next.

"Dawson."

The three men in the sedan slowed up and turned into the parking lot of the small club. The sign on the highway read Little Johnnies Hideaway Club and Motor Cabins. Admittedly they always laughed at the name when they would arrive after pulling a job. Their girls were already there, happily waiting for them in a small room on the other side of the dance floor. There was a small orchestra on a stage to the left with the dance floor in front of you as you walked in, tables to the right and private rooms that were curtained off along the back wall. On the other side of the rooms was a hallway that led to the basement where they had gambling and to a couple of exits just in case you needed to come or go in a hurry. As soon as the three were seated waiters brought them their meal and drinks that the girls had ordered for them long before they had arrived. It was one of Joey's joints that he had picked up somewhere along the way. The only reason he kept it was for just such purposes.

"We were about to give up on you boys," Hope snapped. "You were supposed to have been here hours ago."

"Yeah, Stitchy what took you'se so long," Betty pouted. "You know I don't do so good when yer not around."

She reached up and tried to pull him close for a kiss.

"Aw cut it out Betty," Stitch said pulling away sounding half angry. "How many times I got ta tell ya not in front of da guys?"

"Oh but Stitchy," Betty began but never finished as she noticed the look she was getting from him.

"Come on boys eat up we got some serious dancing to do." Linda the third girl said looking directly at Two Time as she spoke. "You know how I get when I dance."

"Yeah," Shifty laughed, "Drunk."

About an hour after they finished eating the hallway door opened and the big chauffeur pushed his way inside. He made a formidable picture as he filled the doorway with his body. The baseball bat he held in each hand made him that much scarier to look at. His passenger stepped into the room behind him holding a muzzled revolver in each hand. They were both dressed in black head to toe wearing gloves and a mask to hide their faces.

"Ladies take a hike," he said pointing the revolvers squarely at Two Time and Stitch. "Hello boys long time no see."

"Whadaya want," Betty spoke up. "We ain't done nothin. We been here all night wid des guys, ain't we girls? You can even ask Jonese he'll tell ya."

The passenger nodded his head and the chauffeur grabbed her arm and pushed her out into the hallway.

"You two better go too," Shifty told the others. "We'll be alright these guys just wanna talk a little business is all."

"Yeah, that's all," repeated Two Time as he gave Linda a shove.

As the girl went flying toward the intruders he reached for his own gun. Before he could reach it one of the passengers revolvers sounded. Missing Two Time by less than an inch the bullet slammed into the corner of the wall behind him.

"I wouldn't try that again," he said still pointing the revolver at him. "They tell me the bullets in this will rip a hole right through those vests you're wearing like it was butter on a hot August day."

"I believe it," Two Time said turning slightly to look at the hole the bullet had made in the wall behind him. "Whaddya you want wid us?"

"You can tell me what you boys were doing on Thirty-Eighth Street tonight."

"We wasn't anywhere near there," Stitch answered.

The second revolver in the passengers hand sounded. The slug ripped a whole through his chair before burying itself in the wall behind him.

Stitch measured the distance from the hole in his chair to where he'd been sitting using his fingers, gulping unconsciously.

"You boys have only one calling card and you left it all over that street tonight."

"We was there for Tuna," Shifty said finally as if he was bored with the whole game. "He's been trying to break onto that street for the insurance racket; you know the usual thing."

"The old man that ran the pawn shop," Stitch said filling in the pieces. "He's the hold out and the main mouth piece for the shop owners in the neighborhood. Tuna figures if we put a good scare into him they'll come across. So's he hires us and we do what we do."

"That everything?"

"That's it," Two Time added. "Since when've you been so interested in what Tuna does in the insurance business?"

He didn't answer, instead he gave a nod toward the door and the chauffeur backed out of it with his passenger close behind him. Two Time watched them closely as they left something told him that he should follow them out, but as Linda came back into the room he lost all desire to do so. She and the other girls looked so relieved to find out that they still had boyfriends that they quickly dismissed the two intruders as just part of the lifestyle they lived.

In the parking lot the chauffeur found the car the three had used earlier in the night. Smiling the passenger fired the remaining bullets from both revolvers at it. When he finally walked away there were ten holes in the hood of the car. Water was leaking out of the radiator and he thought he even smelled a little oil. Stopping for a second he reloaded one of the revolvers and went to the back of the car. Standing where he could see the gas cap he let the gun pop twice, he could smell the gasoline as it poured out of the tank. As his car pulled up alongside of him he lit three matches together. As he stepped into it he flicked them together toward the smell of gas. The flames from the matches lit the gas fumes and the car was engulfed in fire as they pulled onto the highway.

The sound the car made as the gas in its tank exploded drew everyone out from the club including the three trigger men and their girls. Busboys and waiters ran about the car with fire extinguishers working to put out the fire as some of the club goers cheered them on. Two Time had been decidedly quiet after their visitors had left them. Then all at once something clicked in his head.

"I'll be right back," he told the others as he ran back inside.

Inside the club he went immediately to the phone booths and asked the operator for a number.

"Joey ain't gonna like this one bit," Betty said as she watched the car burn.

"To hell with what Joey likes," Shifty cried. "I finally got that car just the way I wanted it. Oh, man it finally ran perfect and now thanks to him I got to start all over with another car."

The staff at Little Johnnies Hideaway Club and Motor Cabins got the fire put out and everyone went back inside as if it had all been part of the night's entertainment.

When they were far enough away the passenger took off his hat and mask.

"Remind me to call our friend at Smith and Wesson to let him know just how good the new guns he sent me work."

The chauffeur smiled and nodded his head.

"Oh, and don't forget to thank Cook for the box," it was his turn to smile and even chuckle as the chauffeur turned bright red in the dim light of the dashboard.

In his office on the second floor of the Tropic Sun, his downtown night club, Joey sat listening as Two Time told him what had happened. Beginning with what had gone over on Thirty-Eighth Street and not stopping until he told him about the car that had been burning outside the club. He was careful to tell him what he'd seen on the street and the visit they just had received by the two men dressed in black.

Joey knew the two men very well, they had become a huge thorn in his side the way they had been disrupting his enterprise over the past couple of years. He wanted to rub them out, give them cement shoes, make'em sleep with fishes, and he made sure that everyone knew it. The only trouble was he couldn't pin them down to one place. They were like ghosts, no one knew them, and no one knew how they got their information.

Joey "Tuna" Fisher grew up on the docks. His old man was a fisherman. Everyone used to make fun of that fact; Fisher the fisherman. Only Joey wasn't laughing, especially when they began calling him Tuna. His old man fished for tuna and his mother worked in the cannery. Every day of his young life he ate tuna fish. He hated the stuff, but when you're hungry you'll eat whatever is put in front of you and for him it was always tuna. When he was in his teens he threw a fist at anyone that called him by that name. Before he knew it he could take anyone that crossed his path. It was only a matter of time before he offered his services to whoever would pay him. Muscle is muscle and some don't care where it comes from, or what age it is. He started running his first insurance racket by the time he was fifteen. It was about the same time he met Stitch, Two Time and Shifty. The four of them made quite a name for themselves and in a very short time. The only difference was that Joey wanted more. What he couldn't get given to him he took. It wasn't long before Joey was running drugs and a couple of girls. He muscled into his first night club on his twentieth birthday two days later he was the sole owner. Prohibition had only made him even bigger. If it was illegal in the city he had his fingers in it one way or another, from gambling, to drugs, to girls, to guns, to you name it. The standing joke in the city was; that if you wanted it, whatever it was, Joey 'Tuna' Fisher was the one to see about getting it. They still called him Tuna just not always to his face; at least not until his old man's fishing boat had been lost at sea with all hands. From then on he wore the name as a badge of respect for his father.

"Are you sure it was her," he said calmly into the phone.

"As sure as I can be," Two Time replied. "There was no way we could go back and find out."

"Of course not, but if you three idiots hadn't shot up the whole street the cops might not have been crawling around so much."

"We did what you asked," Two Time shouted into the phone.

"Really," Joey shouted back. "Tell me then when did I tell you to shoot the old man that ran that the pawnshop."

"What," his voice was lower now sounded confused. "You said he wouldn't be there. Are you sure it was him?"

"Of course I'm sure; I wouldn't say things like that if I wasn't sure."

Two Time knew that he had his fingers in a lot of pockets and a lot of people in his. He would know everything they knew only hours after they happened. He was sure that this was no different.

"What do you want us to do now?"

"What do I care what you idiots do now," he returned.

"Well you gotta give us a little notice for a few days. We gotta find another car our visitor burned the one we have."

"Yeah," Joey softened remembering what he had been told. "Stay out there for a few days and let things cool off a little. I'm sure the girls won't mind too much. Stretch has a key to my cottage out there. You can stay there. I'll send out a car in couple days to bring you in, unless you can find one out there that fits your needs."

"I'll get shifty to look around and see what comes up."

Joey hung up the phone and poured himself a drink. He went to the window and opened it letting the cool wet air fill the room.

As he took a deep breath of air he could have sworn he smelled the docks. There were a few days that he missed running around bins of ice and fish not many but a few. Some nights he still went down there just to sit and watch them unload the boats. Then again the stuff those boats were unloading often belonged to him. Going back to his desk he picked up the phone receiver and dialed a number.

"I thought you was goin to take care of that problem I been

havin," Joey said into the phone.

"Whadaya mean you still don't know who it is? Isn't that what I pay you for," he said again after listening.

He slammed the receiver back into its cradle before sweeping it and everything else on his desk to the floor.

"I didn't think you cared," Carmen, his current mistress, smiled nervously as she walked into his office.

"What are you doin here?" he asked trying not to let her see his anger.

"Dinner, remember," she walked closer, her legs shook and she hoped he didn't notice.

Joey had a temper everyone knew it and they never knew when that temper was going to end up getting them a bruise or worse.

"I ate hours ago, where were you?"

"I was downstairs at the table waiting for you."

"You should have eaten," he couldn't help but notice how much she looked like Carolyn, something he hadn't really noticed until just then.

Maybe that's why he liked having her around. It certainly wasn't her charm or personality.

"Maybe I shoulda but then you mighta been mad 'cause I started without you. I just never know sometimes." She felt emboldened as she saw him soften more.

She knew the only reason she had any chance with him was because she looked like her. It was something that she took advantage of as often as she could. Like now as she stepped closer and took hold of his arm.

"Come on sweetheart" she said as she began steering him out the door of the office. "Buy me some dinner and then you can show me how much you love me by giving me one of those pretty diamond bracelets you got today."

Joey went along with her without protesting, and laughing as she mentioned the bracelet.

Dawson showed his boredom as he plucked the cherry from

his Manhattan and popped it in his mouth. It was only his third one but on his empty stomach they were quickly working their magic on him. Jane was busy interrogating the young couple about how they had met and their subsequent wedding. A subject he was happy to be ignorant of and had no intention of learning about anytime soon. He happily showed his disinterest by looking around the room. On his third pass he noticed Abrams as he wandered in. Grabbing a couple of cigarettes he quickly excused himself from the table. Catching the detective halfway across the floor he steered him back to the bar.

"You don't wanna go over there," he said taking Abrams by the elbow. "God awful things are being talked about over there."

"Shouldn't I at least say hello?" he asked looking over his shoulder. Then realized that he could be missing out on some evidence he tried to turn around. "They aren't talking about what happened are they?"

"No, no," he said successfully pulling him to the bar. Taking an empty stool he ordered them both a drink. "You see that young couple there?"

"You mean the ones talking to Jane?" he asked before telling the bartender he didn't want anything.

"Yeah that's the one," he returned picking a peanut from the bowl the bartender pushed in front of him as he made their drinks. "They're newlyweds you see and they …"

"Say no more," he said waving his hands back in forth in front of his face. "I decidedly do not want to go over and say hello, even if Jane is better to look at than you."

"I suppose your wife would like to hear you say that."

"Yeah well," the detective started but had no way to finish.

Dawson laughed at his friend and took another peanut.

"You got any idea why they'd want to shot up the pawnshop?" Abrams asked changing the subject knowing that he wouldn't let go of it if he didn't.

"If you don't think they did it for the usual reason then I got nothing new for you."

"You know who it was that invited you?"

"You asked that question once already tonight."

"I thought maybe you might want to change your answer." He picked up Dawson's drink and slugged it back as he waited for an answer.

"I have the note," he replied looking puzzled into his now empty glass. "I am not sure who invited me, I may have an idea who it was but I wouldn't want to share that with you until I know for sure. At least not until I have had a talk with them first."

"Why don't you skip that part and tell me now?"

"Not until I know for sure if they are related or not. If it's not related you don't need to know, but if they are you'll be the first to know after me."

The bartender set another drink in front of Dawson who immediately took hold of it with both hands and took a sip.

"You wanna tell me what you're working on?" Abrams asked him.

"You mean besides this Manhattan and the stale peanuts?" he asked glancing from his drink to his friend and back again.

"Yeah, are you working on something that I should know about," Abrams added just in case there was any question as to what he meant.

"You know better than to accuse me of such a horrible thing."

"So you're not on the job then, no client?"

"Eh," Dawson gave a fake shiver as if something had run up his spine. "Perish the thought. How could you say such things when talking to me?"

"Forgive me," Abrams chuckled, "I should have known better, but somehow I just had to kill the cat."

"I would think there would be much better and quicker ways to kill that cat."

Abrams shook his head as he stood up. He was about to leave before catching a glimpse of the singer sitting at the piano with Jimmy. Tapping Dawson on the shoulder he his shook a thumb in her direction. Dawson closed his left eye in a squint, tipped his head to the right and waggled one hand in front of him as if to say 'not bad'. Jane was too engrossed in conversation with the young couple to notice the movement at the bar.

"Light me a cigarette will ya?" he asked poking one between his lips

"Why can't you do it?" Abrams asked still looking at the singer.

"Well," he returned, still keeping his eyes on his drink. "The last time I let go of my drink with both hands it disappeared and I'm not taking any more chances tonight."

"Looks like you need a lighter." Abrams said patting him on the shoulder and leaving the bar.

Dawson shook his head and called the bartender over. Smiling he saw his dilemma and quickly lit the cigarette dangling from his mouth. Setting the pack of matches in front of him, he shook his head and smiled as he walked away. Sighing as he exhaled Dawson let go of his drink with one hand, but just long enough to remove the cigarette from his lips. Keeping the glass solidly between both hands he returned to his table as the waiter brought them their supper.

"Hey," he said stopping the waiter. "Don't go anywhere."

The waiter looked puzzled but stopped anyway without questioning him.

"I am sure he's a very busy man," Jane said in the waiter's defense. "Besides why do you need him there anyway?"

"I let go of my drink two times in this clip joint and both times they disappeared," Dawson said still holding his drink. "I want him to keep one hand on it while I have something to eat or feed me my dinner. I haven't really decided yet which would be the best approach."

"But Dawson," Jane added.

"Yeah you're probably right," he replied shooing the waiter away with his head. "I'm going to have to re-think this. Come back in two minutes and check on me to make sure no one stole another one of my drinks."

"Whatever you say sir," the waiter chuckled backing away

from the table.

"What happened to the …," he said waving one hand at the two empty chairs.

"Oh," she said catching on, "They're doing something I can never get you to do; they're dancing."

"Eh, dancing, whoever invented it should be drawn and quartered. At the very least keel hauled."

"I don't think they had those things then."

"You could always ask your mother; she's old enough, she might know."

"Dawson!"

He laughed to himself as he lifted his fork and tore into his supper forgetting, for a time, his drink. By the time the young couple had returned to the table he had finished his main course and was thinking of dessert.

"Amaretto," he finally told the waiter. "And make it rough."

As he disappeared the singer stepped up to their table.

"Mr. Dawson," she said as she got close enough. "Mr. Dawson, my name is Maria Leonard. I, well I really need to talk to you if you have a minute."

Looking up he was a little upset for being interrupted, but the moment he saw who it was he forgave her, telling her that he had all the time she needed.

"Jimmy tells me that you find things, people I mean," she said. "I was wondering what it would take for you to help me."

"That depends on what you want me, rather who you want me to find," he added sipping his drink before popping a cigarette between his lips.

"Well you see I don't have much money," she began, "and well Jimmy says that sometimes a person can owe you and that you'll work it out with them."

Watching them as he played Jimmy tossed his head back giving him a wink as if to say she was being straight with him.

"Why don't you come see me tomorrow," Dawson returned nodding back at him. "Then you can fill me in on who it is that you want me to find and I'll tell you what you'll owe me."

Smiling she kissed him on the cheek before returning to the stage. Jane hadn't been oblivious to the encounter not that she could have been if she tried. Although she did her best not trip the girl as she walked passed her.

"Oh Dawson," she said batting her eyes like a bad movie actress. "I will so ever be in your debt; hogwash."

"Now Jane your claws are showing," he returned. "Bad kitty; mustn't let the other kitties see them. Besides I am sure that she is just a poor innocent lamb that has lost her wool."

"Oh, Dawson," she sighed shaking her head.

Edward "Pop" Morre lay asleep in the hospital bed as the officer on duty closed the door and walked to the nurse's station. He watched as the duty nurse looked over several patient charts. She was closer to sixty than she was forty, and by his estimate had seen better days. She may have been pretty at one time but the long hours of being on her feet taking care of others had taken their toll in an unfriendly way. She looked tired and mean, and as far as he was concerned he was being kind.

"He gonna be alright?"

The desk nurse looked up confused at first who the officer was talking about but soon enough remembered the gunshot patient in the room up the hall.

"Doctor says if he makes it through the night he should be just fine." she said looking back to the chart she was holding.

"Well," he added, "I don't take much stock in what they have to say. What do you nurses think?"

"I honestly wouldn't have thought he would have lasted this long so I wouldn't trust my thoughts on the matter at all."

As the officer was about to leave the desk another nurse came around the corner.

"You find the one responsible for shooting Mr. Morre?" she asked as she reached the desk.

"Not yet," he returned quickly half looking for an escape from the desk.

"I hope you find them soon it makes a girl feel unsafe every time they bring in one of them shooting victims."

"I am sure it won't be too long," he added finally turning to look at her. "Well, hello sister."

He figured she stood a bit over five six, with wire framed glasses that only tended to highlight her green eyes, and even with her blonde hair pulled up and back he could tell she was a girl that all the guys paid attention to when she walked by.

"Well hello yourself," she giggled. "You're not so bad to look at either. Tall dark and in uniform, just the way I like'em"

"You two better take your foot off the gas, and put it in neutral. It's going to be a long night Nurse Simon," the older nurse told them. "As for you Officer … Officer Jacks you should be over there by that door and not standing around here making trouble."

The Officer went back to his post but not without looking over his shoulder more than once at Nurse Simon.

Abrams sat next to his shooting victim writing a few notes on the off chance that he would have more paperwork than he wanted to do. It was much easier, at least in his mind, to do the paperwork for a living victim than a dead one. Although even if he wouldn't admit it, he often changed his mind, especially when the dead were themselves murderers. He slipped into the room when Jacks was talking to the nurses. Making a little side note he reminded himself to take a chunk out of the young officers hide as soon as he could do so privately at least. He didn't see any reason to embarrass him in front of the women. Satisfied that Morre would sleep through the rest of the night he left the room carefully as not to disturb him. As he opened the door he found Jacks in his chair leaning back against the wall. All thoughts of waiting to reprimand the officer in private went out the window as he watched him begin to read a newspaper. With one swift kick he pushed the chairs legs out from under the officer causing it to collapse in a pile of useless wood as Jacks landed on top of it.

"You've just been told off," he said as Jacks came up ready

to take a swing. "Next time you leave your post even if it's just to shake one off check and make sure what you're guarding is still there when you get back."

Jacks turned thirty shades of red as the nurses came around their station at the sound of the breaking chair.

"You could have killed him with a stunt like that," the older nurse scolded as checked him over.

"That was exactly the point I wanted to get across," Abrams stated ignoring the tone the nurse used toward him.

Walking away he tipped his hat to Nurse Simon, who had her hand over her mouth and was laughing as quietly as she could manage. On his way out of the hospital he stopped at a phone booth and made a call.

She woke with a start unsure of her surroundings. It took her several seconds before she realized where she was. Letting out a sigh she collapsed back on the large bed. Pulling the fluffy blankets back up over her she closed her eyes and hoped for more sleep.

"Good morning Miss Carolyn," Jamie called as she entered the room. Going straight for the curtains she pulled them back away from the windows letting in the morning sun.

Carolyn sighed from somewhere deep under the big fluffy bed spread.

"Did you sleep good 'nuf Miss Carolyn?"

"Jamie how many times have I tried to tell you," she began tossing the blankets off her. "There is no such word as 'nuf."

"I sorry Miss Carolyn you know I never see'd the inside of no school afore," Jamie giggled knowing that the woman was teasing her more than upset for saying the word. "My momma says I lucky ah 'nuf to speak a tall."

"I thought the mister was going to send you to some classes."

"He were aw right," Jamie returned as she handed her a robe. "But, you know what, my man say I talk jus fine for him and dat I don't be needin no classes in how ta talk like you."

She smiled at the maid and gave her a quick hug before asking where her clothes were. Opening the wardrobe the maid waved her arm in front of the open doors as she turned and left the room.

"Ahem," the maid started as she stopped just outside the bedroom door. "Breakfast will be ready by the time you are dressed."

Jamie smiled as she spoke and gave a little flourish of her hands when she finished. Carolyn couldn't help but laugh, applauding silently.

"How'd I do dat time Miss," Jamie giggled again.

"Wonder-fully," she replied still applauding. "But you bes get back to da ketchen a fore yo momma start a wonderin where you be."

With that Jamie couldn't help but to bust into full robust laughter as she turned and walked away.

Sitting on the edge of the bed Carolyn scolded herself for being so cheerful just hours after Pop had been shot and killed.

"All because of me," she whispered as tears once again began to well up in her eyes.

A knock on the bedroom door brought her back to reality.

"Are you decent?" he asked through the door.

"Always for you Darling," she answered wiping her eyes. "Come in."

She stood up still half naked as the door was open. Running to him she landed between his outstretched arms hiding her face in his chest.

"I am sorry I wasn't here when you arrived," he said as he wrapped his arms tightly around her. "Jamie had said that you were in the bath when I got back, but I thought it best to wait until this morning to welcome you properly."

"I could have used these arms around me last night just as well as today."

"The staff talks enough when you're here as it is," he chuckled. "Just think what they would be saying if I had gone into your bath."

"Since when were you ever afraid of what your staff said about me or the other women that have been in your home?"

He sat in one of the rooms plush chairs pulling her to him. Kneeling in front of him she placed her head against his chest again before telling him everything that had happened the night before. He didn't say a word as she spoke. When she finished he stood up pulling her in close to him again. They stood for several seconds locked together in the middle of the room. Looking up at him she seemed desperate for him to lean in and kiss her. Instead he turned her around told her to finish dressing and gave her naked bottom a quick slap.

"Now that wasn't very gentlemanly of you," she screeched excitedly as his hand struck its intended target.

"Whatever gave you the impression that I was gentlemanly," he laughed. "Just because I come from a 'good' family doesn't mean that they taught me to be that gentlemanly. Besides you always bring out the ungentlemanly side of me."

"If I believe that you won't try to sell me a bridge somewhere will you?" she asked sarcastically

"Just finish getting dressed," he returned as he left the room. "I'll be down on the patio when you're ready. Such a great morning I thought we'd have breakfast outside."

Standing where he'd left her she rubbed her bottom where he had slapped it. She was far from being prudish and it wasn't as if he hadn't seen her naked before, but something in his slap told her that he wasn't the same man she used to know. Then again she wasn't the same woman she had been two years earlier either. All she could do now was tell him everything and hope that he would forgive her. Although, she thought, there wasn't much chance of that once he knew her past.

Douglas Barnes, attorney at law, retired, but not by his own choice, was young, tall and lean. He'd been born to money and was handsome enough for most of the women that had the pleasure to meet him. He wore his dark brown hair cut a little closer than most of the men his age, a habit he had picked up after he'd spent time in the Army. A semi chiseled chin and light brown eyes finished out his looks. Making him popular enough about town that more than one woman had their hook baited for him.

Sitting at the table he picked up the morning paper, which by this time was hours old. There was a write up about the shooting but there was no mention that Pop had been shot and of course nothing about her. He smiled; glad that he at least wouldn't have to explain anything to his family, for now anyway. He decided that he would have to make sure it stayed that way.

"Good morning sir," Harold, his butler, said as he set the coffee urn next to him.

Harold had come with the house that he inherited from his Grandfather. He was born in London and trained as a true English butler at the age of fifteen. He had traveled to America at the age of twenty-two after being hired by a family to look after their newlywed son that was taking a position in the families New York office. After disaster stuck the young couple, they'd both been killed by a mugger, he was in affect stranded. That is until the late Mr. Masters took him on and he had been happily working for the family ever since.

He bid the servant a curt good morning before telling him that he needed to instruct the rest of the staff not to tell anyone about their visitor. He nodded as he left him on the patio.

Douglas had always tried to be friendly with his staff, he had never liked the way his family had sometimes treated them as he grew up. He knew there was a line that he should not cross as well as a class distinction between them. However, he demanded that there be as few barriers between himself and his own staff as possible. That is all except Harold who had insisted that they not get too close or too friendly. Although truth be told there was a great bond of friendship between them as well as mutual respect and understanding.

"Do I look presentable enough for you now?" she asked as she walked out on to the patio. "I can always change if you don't like it."

Smiling he noticed that she had decidedly not finished

dressing. Instead she chose to wear a short silk robe that she had worn on other occasions. Kissing him on the cheek before sitting down across the table from him she tried her best to be cheery. Handing her the morning paper he couldn't help but smile again as he remembered the last time that she had stayed with him.

"Darling," he said lifting his nose in the air and trying to sound stuffy. "I do believe you wore that same outfit the last time you came. Don't you own anything else?"

"I could take it off if you wish," she giggled lifting her hands teasingly to her shoulders.

"Don't you dare," he snapped back, "that's all we would need to happen."

Looking back at him she produced her best pouty face before sticking her tongue out at him.

"Spoil sport," she added finally.

The color drained from her face as she read and re-read the story that Tiny had written for The Globe. She looked again for any mention of Pop getting shot, the only names she could find were the names of the owners of the stores that had been hit with bullets and his name wasn't there either.

"I don't understand," she added several times as she kept looking over the story.

"I wouldn't worry about it, I'm sure it's something the police wanted to keep out of the papers so that they could investigate more easily."

"You would know better than I would I suppose," she said looking reassured.

"One would think that you were disappointed by not reading about a murder in the papers this morning."

"You're right darling," she returned. "I guess I just hoped that maybe he wasn't dead and that they would tell that if it were true."

"What would you like to do today?" he asked changing the subject, trying to reassure her that everything was going to be all right.

"I have a few ideas," she answered smiling and touching the front of her robe.

"A few more of those ideas and I'm quite sure we'll both be in trouble with someone."

"Tell me then," she began; her face full of disappointment. "Just who is it that belongs to those clothes upstairs?"

He looked at her over the top of the paper he was reading before burying his nose back in it.

"Are you pleading the fifth counselor?"

"Nope," he replied not looking up. "I'm just formulating my answer."

"I see," she was visibly hurt by his answer, but she didn't know why.

She hadn't seen him in nearly two years so it wasn't as if she still had any claims to him. She'd always wanted to have that claim, but that was before Joey found out she knew him. At first she vowed to weather the storm of his ruined career, but when Joey began to threaten to attack him using her past everything changed. After taking her home from a date one night she packed her things and disappeared. There had been a note to explain why she'd left. At least she wrote it, he just never got it. That wasn't good enough for Joey though, he kept threatening to use her past against him. That is until she agreed to become his mistress. After that she was in her own downward spiral for nearly a year. Joey had kept his word but being with him wasn't easy for her. In his world everything and anything came and went at the snap of his fingers. She was drunk most of the time for the first few months just to make it easier. After that she turned to some of the girls for extra help, they gave her cocaine from there it was an easy walk to heroin. It wasn't being with Joey that made her turn to the candy. After all she'd grown up poor. Hunger will do things to some that it may not do to another. Everything she had done in her past made it easy for the way Joey treated her. She'd known men like him since she was fourteen. The drugs were supposed to help her forget him, except she would never be able forget Douglas. After getting away from Joey she told herself that she'd never see either of them again. Only that didn't seem to be working very well. She'd moved every couple of months after that. Each time changing her name trying to distance herself from the name she'd used before. With her latest move she remembered thinking how funny it would be if Douglas knew that she was using his grandfather's last name.

As hard as she tried hiding from him she wasn't surprised when he came into the nightclub two months earlier with a blonde on his arm. She had met the girl when she was seeing him, but she couldn't remember her name. If he'd seen her when he walked in he didn't show it. Not that she was trying to hide from him there. That is unless staring at him all night could be considered hiding. An hour later while his date was in the powder room he walked over to her table. Leaning over he whispered in her ear and placed the matchbook with his number on it in her hand. As he walked away her new friends gave her a hard time about having a strange man giving her his number. Playing along she told them that it happened all the time. Certainly, she'd told them, it must happen to them all the time. Disagreeing they told her that it didn't happen to them; ever. Much to her friends dismay she made a big deal about throwing the number away. In reality she couldn't do it. Instead she had secretly slipped it into her bag. She had finally shaken herself free from the cocaine and the heroin just a month before seeing him. Maybe she'd only kept his number because she was still weak. However, she knew that she would never be strong enough where he was concerned.

Now he was back her life; something that she wanted, but knew she couldn't have. There was no way that she would be able to stay in it especially if Joey found out. There was no telling what he would do to her or him when he did. You didn't end anything with Joey unless he ended it. When he was through with you, you knew it and chances were good that you ended up in the river or in one of his houses with an arm full of heroin for you troubles.

"Have you formulated your answer yet counselor?" she asked as she finished the last of her breakfast.

"You aren't going to believe this," he started, getting up from chair and walking to her. "They're yours."

"You're right," she laughed, "I don't believe you."

"I figured you wouldn't believe me," he said taking her hand.

"But it's true. I ordered them for you. They've been sitting in that wardrobe for two years waiting for you to come back."

"But Douglas you didn't live here then."

"That's true, however that is the same wardrobe that was in your room at the old house." He tried not to sound melancholy but it wasn't easy. "I wanted to surprise you the next time you came to visit. Remember when my mother came and you cried for hours because you didn't have anything nice enough to wear. You were afraid mother would think you too common and not good enough for her boy."

"If I remember correctly, I was right; she didn't like me at all." She remembered the night all too well, along with the looks that she gave her every time she spoke.

"Yes, well," he continued trying not to think of his mother. "The next day I had Jamie get all the information needed to be able to buy you a full wardrobe. There are at least three outfits for every occasion up in your room."

Lifting her from her chair he held her hands tight. Looking down at her body she noticed how much weight she had lost in two years. There was little doubt in her mind what had caused her to lose it. She was determined to gain most of it back and to never let what happened to her happen again. Pushing herself into him she didn't wait for him to kiss her as she pressed her lips to his.

"Horseback riding," he said as she pulled away.

"Horseback riding," she said. "After a kiss like that all you can say is horseback riding?"

"Sure, I'll call the stables and have them saddle our horses and we'll go riding."

"You sure know how to hurt a girl," she added, "especially

after she's just thrown herself at you."

A tear formed in the corner of her eyes and she turned her face away from him.

"Just formulating my answer your honor," he returned, turning her back to face him and kissing her deeply.

Dawson lay where he had fallen, half-dressed across his bed. He'd finally reached it sometime after five in the morning, beating the milkman, but only by a couple of minutes. The incessant sound of the door buzzer finally woke him. Sleepily he reached for the phone. Saying hello he listened for a few seconds before tossing the receiver over the edge of the bed. He put his head back down and ignored the buzzer figuring that he was only dreaming. A minute later Abrams stood over his bed. Picking up his arm he put his fingers on his pulse.

"Nope," he chuckled, "you're still alive."

Dawson grumbled something in his half sleep.

"Yeah, yeah, just get up," he added giving him a shove.

Lifting his head finally he squinted and looked at his torturer.

"That's it sleepy head time to get up."

"Go away, I'm dreaming."

"Too bad," he returned grabbing his arm and rolling him on his side.

"So you're a dream hater now." He was a bit groggy and his voice was rough, but he was waking up.

"You always leave your door unlocked?" he asked when he was sure he had as much of his attention as possible for the moment.

Rubbing his head between his hands he rolled the rest of the way over. Keeping a hand on each side of his head he stared up at the ceiling.

"Was I supposed to meet you somewhere?" he asked finally.

"Nope, I just needed to see your smiling hangover and I had a question for you as well."

"Then you better let me get a drink first."

Crawling off his bed he ever so slowly shuffled out of his

bedroom. Abrams chuckled and followed him into the living room. Grabbing a bottle of Irish whisky he held it to his head for a few seconds feeling the cool glass. Pouring the drink he turned back to his friend.

"Alright, do your worse," he groaned before falling into an ugly large overstuffed chair.

"You sure you didn't leave anything out last night when you told me what happened?"

He snapped back the jigger of whiskey and poured another one before answering.

"What are you trying to get at?"

"I'm asking if you saw anyone else last night at the time of the shooting."

Thinking for a second he downed the drink and looked at his friend. It wasn't so much that he wanted to protect Sally. It was more that he was sure that she had nothing to do with Pop getting shot that he hesitated.

"You think I'm not shooting straight with you or what?"

"You know me Dawson just trying to cover the bases."

"You're right I know you and you don't ask a question like that without reason. That means you have another witness and they saw someone else, that about right."

"Never could pull that one on you," he returned half laughing. "It was worth the try, seeing as you're hung over and all."

Dawson knew that he was fishing, but who he was fishing for was the question of the day.

"Well," he started; throwing him a bone to see where he buried it. "I did see someone before the shooting they may have seen the car but I am sure they didn't have anything to do with it."

"What makes you sure?"

"First of all they weren't carrying a Chicago typewriter. Second of all they weren't around at the time of the shooting."

"How's that?"

"They walked past before the shooting. By the time the car came round the corner they were walking up a flight of stairs on the opposite side of the street if you must know."

"And you don't know who it was?"

"How would I know that; I don't live in that neighborhood."

"You'd know Sally Masters if you saw her wouldn't you?"

"Name doesn't ring a bell," he knew he shouldn't lie to his friend any more than he had to, but there was something in the way he asked that bothered him. "Who was it that saw her?"

"Riley says that one of the neighbors saw her in front of the pawnshop when the car went by."

"Really," he replied holding back a chuckle. "Do you think that if she was in front of that pawnshop when the car went by she wouldn't have still been there in a pool of blood after they went around the other corner?"

"I had thought of that, but you know me, I had to ask just the same."

"How about we get some breakfast and you can fill me in on anything I don't know about since I was there."

"Breakfast," Abrams laughed. "It's way past breakfast time my friend."

Dawson took a quick shower and was dressed with in fifteen minutes. Remembering to lock his door, they left his apartment and went to the delicatessen a couple of blocks away.

"How's the wife anyway?" Dawson asked as they sat down.

"How do you suppose," he returned, "she's a cop's wife."

"Miserable on the inside but puts up a good front, yeah I know how they are."

With the help of his trusty flask full of Irish whisky that he was pouring liberally into his coffee Dawson was quickly getting past his hangover. As they ate the two talked about little things that pertained to nothing as only friends can.

"Did Jane get anything of those newlyweds to rub off on you last night?" he asked knowing that the woman would try almost anything to land him at the altar.

"If she had," Dawson smiled smugly, "do you think you would have found me alone in that bed?"

"If I remember correctly…" Abrams began.

"Never mind finishing that remembrance Chester."

After downing the remainder of his third cup of coffee he stuck a cigarette between his lips. He was about to light it when something out on the street caught his attention. Holding the lit match he nearly burned his fingers before Abrams voice snapped him back to reality. He quickly lit his cigarette on what was left of the burning match before tossing it in the ashtray. Excusing himself he went over to the window. Out on the street he recognized two of Tuna's goons as they were going in and out of businesses. Shaking his head he went back to the table. Abrams asked him what was up, but all he said was to wait and see. About a minute later the two made their way into the delicatessen. Giving a nod he pointed out the two he'd seen in the street to his friend. Confused Abrams watched as they walked up to the owner, it took him a few seconds to realize what was happening. Standing, he made his way slowly toward the cash register where the three had congregated. Slipping his hand around to the holster in the middle of his back he pulled his service revolver. One of the men slapped the owner across the face as Abrams pistol came to bear on them. Dawson was still at the table but already had one of his automatics out ready to back him up.

"I wouldn't do that again if I were you," Abrams called to them.

"What do you care what we do," one of the goon's answered back.

Dawson did a duck walk as he moved around behind the counter to get a better angle on them.

"I guess you didn't hear me," he returned waving his revolver back and forth getting them to see it better.

"I guess you don't know who we are," said the other goon reaching for his heater.

"Touch that rod and you're a dead man," called Dawson leveling his pistol at the second man. "Then it won't matter who you are."

"Since when is dis any of yer business Dawson?" the first

goon asked recognizing him.

"Please gentlemen," the owner began with a heavy German accent, pleading with all of them. "No violence, please no one needs to get hurt I give them their money and they go away."

"There's not going to be any violence," Abrams added, "is there boys?"

"Not if you back away and let us get out of here, we'll forget the whole thing if you do."

"I don't think that's going to happen do you Dawson," Abrams returned.

"Me, why are you asking me," he replied, "up until a couple of seconds ago I was just an innocent bystander."

The rest of the customers who had been enthralled with what was happening were beginning to show signs of nervousness. They were ducking under tables everywhere when they began to realize that someone was probably about to get shot.

Abraham Dershowitz was a heavy set man in his late fifties or early sixties depending on who you talked to. He and his wife Stella had emigrated from Germany fifteen years earlier. They bought the delicatessen just three days later. They had no children, but they were always helping the ones in the neighborhood. Feeding them when they looked hungry, even giving some of them jobs. His employees had always been children from the neighborhood. When you worked there he and his wife made sure that you went to school every day and always took home something to eat for your family. His wife died just a few years earlier, and he still worked behind the counter every day from open to close. He was the first one to arrive and the last one to leave. There were many times that he never made it home and could be found asleep in the basement while he waited on a delivery.

"No, no, no," Abraham pleaded again but this time in his native German, "Please, please, no violence."

He was frustrated. His face turning beat red as he slipped back into his native language.

"Everything is going to be fine," Dawson returned in his best German, trying to calm him down. "I promise."

Abraham smiled at him looking surprised. The two goons turned and looked at him as well. Giving Abrams just time enough to get a step closer. However it wasn't enough as the second goon drew his gun while the first pulled Abraham closer to use as a shield. The second goons automatic barked but missed its mark. Abrams revolver answered hitting the man square in the chest. The force of the bullet knocked him back against the wall. His eyes were wide open in shock as he slipped to the floor. The remaining goon moved toward the door keeping Abraham in front of him as a shield. Abrams turned quickly to face the first one.

"I got him," Dawson said taking another step to his left.

Raising his automatic higher until it pointed at the goons head he spoke to Abraham again in German. This time telling him to push back against the man quickly and then to fall forward. The scared red faced man nodded quickly and did as he was told. Before Tuna's boy could react Dawson fired. The bullet hit its intended target high on his left shoulder spinning him around before he fell groaning in pain. Abraham turned white as he looked at the man on the floor behind him.

"Better get an ambulance," Abrams said as he looked over their handy work.

"Can you boys help Mr. Dershowitz?" Dawson asked as he picked up his spent shell.

They nodded and three of them went to their bosses side and helped him up and over to a chair.

"This one's not going to be much help," Abrams said finally after checking them both. "I guess my aim is off today I only meant to wing him."

"I guess mine is too," Dawson added as he looked down at the one he'd shot. "I was trying to put it between his eyes."

The man groaned as his eyes rolled back in his head and passed out. Most probably because of the pain, although they were sure that finding out that he should have been dead didn't help.

"You know these two?" Abrams asked

"Only by site, but I know who they work for."

"Joey 'Tuna'," Abrams said easily as he handcuffed the two men together.

One of the boys from behind the counter walked up and pointed them out.

"That one there," he said pointing to the dead one. "That one is Bradley King, that other one is Mike Calluchi."

"You mean Mike 'the Nose'," Dawson asked.

The kid who couldn't have been more than eleven or twelve nodded before going to look after his boss.

"Well ain't that co-inky-dink," he laughed as he looked closer at the passed out man.

"You gotta help him," one of the boys yelled excitedly.

Turning they noticed that Dershowitz was having trouble breathing.

"Looks like he's having a heart attack," Dawson said finally. "There's a doctor on the next street over if you ...."

One of the boys was out the door before he could finish.

"His ticker ain't so good," one of the older boys added.

"Pills," he managed to say, again in German, pointing to the counter.

The boys all flew to the counter to look for them. Finding the pills they gave them to Dershowitz. It looked to Abrams and Dawson that they had done it before and were happy that they knew what to do. Sirens in the distance sounded the coming of the ambulance and no doubt a police car or two. It wasn't long before the boy who had left returned with a pretty redhead in tow carrying a medical bag.

"This isn't Doc Dennison," Dawson said shaking his head.

"I'm his daughter," she returned quickly running over to Dershowitz. "Hello Abraham."

She knelt in front him and began listening to his heart. The boys told her that they had just given him one of his pills.

"Nitro?" she stated more than asked.

He nodded trying to slow his breathing. The ambulance stopped out front and soon the place was filled with cops and bystanders. Abrams took charge and had the officers clear the shop except for the people that needed to be there. The older boys in the shop took charge of the rest of them and sent them back to work cleaning up.

"They are good boys," Dershowitz said as they immediately began clearing tables and making the store ready again for customers.

Dawson had to agree as he watched them. He had eaten there often over the years and known some of the boys. He made a mental note to keep an eye on the place for a few days at the very least.

As the ambulance doctor worked on the Mike 'the Nose,' Abrams leaned over and pressed a few questions to him.

"Where were you last night?"

"Drop off copper," Mike returned. "I ain't tellin you nuttin' an you'se can't make me."

"You're one of Joey's boys aren't you?"

"Never hoid of 'em."

"You mean if I went and asked the business owners on the street who you were collecting for they would say no one?"

"Dey betta tell you'se I ain't collectin for no one or I'll kill'em," Mike yelled loud enough so that everyone could hear him.

"You're a three time loser Mike," Dawson said looking at him. "Even the Bureau boys want you for killing one of their own."

"They ain't got nuttin. You gonna get me outta here so'se I don't have ta look at dis chump." He returned pointing his left thumb toward the dead body of his partner.

"Nah," Dawson chimed in. "I think you need to sit there for a while so that you can see what'll happen to you if anyone comes here to keep collecting for 'no one'."

"You'se threatin me or sumptin'" Mike returned becoming more visibly angry.

"I guess I am Mikey, I guess I am."

"You can't do dat," Mike shook from his anger as he spoke

this time. "Get me outta des nippers I'll kill you right here."

"You'll be dead before you can blink if you try."

"Yeah," Mike began again, "You'se can't threaten me like dat. Hey copper tells him he can't threaten me like dat."

"I didn't hear a thing," Abrams smiled and turned to another officer. "You hear anything Officer?"

"Who me sir," the officer replied. "Was I supposed to be listening to you or something? I'm sorry sir there was some piece of garbage in the corner whining about being hurt. I promise I'll pay better attention in the future sir."

"Wait'll I tell my mouth piece what you'se done Dawson. You'se won't be such a big shot den I tell ya."

"Can we take him to the hospital now," the doctor asked.

"You got everything you need?" Abrams asked his crime boys.

They all nodded that they did.

The doctor looked and waited for him to take the handcuffs off him but he didn't. Instead he ordered the wounded man and another officer to carry the body of Bradley King to the ambulance and load them together to go to the hospital.

"You can tell them I made you do it," Abrams turned away as Mike started complaining again.

"You'se can't make me ride in da same wagon as a stiff you'se can't do that."

"Now, now, Mikey," the officer that was holding up one side of Bradley Kings body told him. "Money's tight with the city. You know we can't afford to be sending out two meat wagons just to pick up the trash."

"Is he going to be all right?" Dawson asked turning to Dershowitz and the redhead.

"I'm going to take him to the hospital," she said still looking at her patient. "I want to keep him there for a day or two just to be on the safe side."

"No, No, No," he insisted still in his native German. "I won't go. I cannot go, who will look after the store? Who will look after the boys?"

"I will Abraham," said a young man about twenty two as he walked through the door. "You do what the doctor says. I will come and look after the store and the boys."

"But Daniel what of your good job," Dershowitz shook his head nearly in tears at the sight of him. "We work so hard to get that job. No you cannot, I will not allow it you must not worry about us here you must worry only about you."

Daniel had been under Abraham's feet from day one. He'd only given him a job because he couldn't get rid of him. It was a week before he found out that the boy had no parents, nowhere to go, and no idea what his last name was. His wife made the boy stay with them and on his next birthday, a day he picked, they gave him their last name. He was the first of the many children they helped over the years. He didn't want to but they even made him go to school every day. Then they made sure he went to college.

"Don't worry if they fire me I will get an even better job," he said taking Abraham's face between his hands. "Besides isn't that what a son is supposed to do?"

The two hugged and he could no longer hold back the tears.

It was a touching scene and nearly everyone in the room showed signs of tearing. Even the cynical Dawson had to step outside to avoid it. Lighting a cigarette as soon as he hit the sidewalk he began looking up and down the street. A thought struck him as he tossed his match to the gutter. Calling one of the officers over he told him what he was thinking.

"You know wherever these two came from it's a safe bet they didn't walk here," he began. "How about you get a couple of boys and start looking at all the cars up and down the street. I didn't hear anyone taking off after the shots. I'm pretty sure if they had a wheelman he'd have torn out of here pretty fast. Don't you agree?"

The officer was a bit old for a beat cop. He was sixty if he was a day. He was lean with a face that had seen its fair share of knuckles and then some. His nose was flat and big from being broken more than a couple of times. In spite of the hard features of his face his blue eyes looked soft and kind.

"I think you might be right there Dawson," he said patting him on the back. "It's too bad you didn't join up, you'd've made a great copper."

"Oh, I don't know," he returned. "I don't think I done so bad. Some think I'm a pretty good copper without having joined up."

The two laughed as the officer went to gather a couple of boys to search the cars still on the street.

"I would ask a few of the other shop owners too in case they spotted them getting out of it," he called to him as he walked away.

The officer waved his hand in the air as he walked away to acknowledge that he heard him.

"What's going on?" Abrams asked as he followed the wounded and dead out of the shop.

He filled him in on his thought and what he had done. He agreed with him that it was worth looking for it on the off chance it had been the same car that had pulled the job the night before.

"That's why I make the big bucks." He added flicking his cigarette into the gutter then fished in his pocket for another. "That tears it Chester I'm out of smokes."

Abrams laughed as he grabbed a cigarette from one of the bystanders and handed it to him.

"I think I'll go find some cigarettes," he said allowing his friend to light the one he had just given him. "You done here?"

"I don't think so," he replied. "I'll catch up to you later if I can."

Dawson shook his friends hand and walked away in his search for cigarettes. Grabbing his flask he shook it only to find out it too was empty.

"Ah, what a sad end of a good hangover cure and it's wearing off as well," he said aloud as he walked.

He bought a newspaper and a pack of cigarettes from a corner newsstand a few blocks down. Counting himself lucky he crossed the street to a bar on opposite corner. The sign over the door said it was the Boulevard Bar and Grille. He remembered it had been just a Grille with a speakeasy in the basement during the nasty little dry spell. He was happy to see they had joined the two up when it got wet again.

It was late afternoon and there were only a few customers in the bar and a few of them were sitting around at tables eating. He took off his hat set it in front of him on the bar and waited for the bartender. Opening his pack of cigarettes he read the front page of the paper. He didn't look up when the bartender asked him what he wanted. Taking a cigarette out of the pack he told him he wanted a bourbon and soda.

"Sure thing Mr. Dawson," the bartender replied.

He finally looked up and tried to place the face.

"Ah, I'm sure you don't remember me," he added pouring his drink. "You pinched me a while back on a rap. I was only sixteen then so I doubt you remember me."

"You're right can't say's I do at the moment," he said exhaling smoke.

He scratched his head and admitted to having a hangover.

"Oh sure," the bartender laughed. "Well I got the cure for that."

He set his drink in front of him and introduced himself again.

"Patrick Graham," he said sticking out his hand. "You pinched me trying to rob a warehouse down on the wharf."

"Yes," Dawson acknowledged taking his outstretched hand. "'Kid Pat', you fell through a sky light and broke both your legs right?"

"Yeah," Graham replied sheepishly, lowering his head. "That was me alright. I got three to five for that rap had to do all five, thanks to you; been straight ever since I got out though. Well, ever since it got wet anyway. Got me a pretty little wife and a beautiful baby girl too."

He went to the end of the bar and came back with a picture of his wife and baby. Dawson looked at the picture and tried to see the resemblance between the proud papa and the baby. He didn't see any, but at least she looked enough like her mother that he'd probably never ask the question.

Patrick 'Kid Pat' Graham was an average looking kid in his early twenties, blonde hair, and grey eyes. He was thin, but he had enough muscle showing that you wouldn't mistake him for someone unable to take care of them self. Walks with a limp if he's on his feet too long. A left over from his fall through the skylight. Dawson caught him on the roof and it was his own stupidity that caused the fall. Still he considered himself lucky to have been caught just the same. It turned his life around and in fact he'd met his wife while in prison.

"Too bad about the shooting last night," he said after he handed him back his photograph. "Pop's an alright guy. He gives it to you square. I used to try and get him to buy my stuff once in a while but he was pretty smart, always knew when I had hot merchandise. Bought the wife's engagement ring from him. A few other things too I'm not too proud to say. Yeah, shame they had to shoot him."

"You know anything about it?" Dawson asked taking a long swig of his drink.

"Nah, not really," he returned almost sounding as if he realized he might have said too much. "Just a bunch of gossip from here you know how it is, everyone thinks they know everything in a bar."

Dawson raised his glass as if to toast the statement.

He was on is second drink when two men and a woman walked into the bar. They were talking about what had happened at the delicatessen.

"It was the cop that killed the one gangster," said the tallest of the men as he hung his hat on the rack attached to the booth.

"Where you there?" the woman asked excitedly.

"Nah, my secretary was though," he said sliding into the seat.

"You think it had anything to do with the shooting on Thirty-Eighth Street last night?" the shorter man asked hanging his and the woman's overcoats on the rack.

"I doubt it," the woman said as she slipped in the booth across from the first man.

The shorter man hung his hat with their coats and slid in next to the woman and took her hand for a second under the table.

It wasn't hard for Dawson to hear them the place had cleared out and they weren't exactly whispering.

"My secretary told me the dead guy was Bradley King and the wounded guy was Mike 'The Nose'." He paused and lit a cigarette and thought for a second.

"I heard the owner had a heart attack and nearly died." The woman said excited to be able to add to conversation.

"She also seemed to think that the other guy that did the shooting was that Dawson guy," the tall guy began again. "But I told her that couldn't be. I heard that he's been out of town for a long time, so there's no way he was there."

"Hey those two guys work for that gangster everyone calls Joey Tuna, don't they," the shorter man chimed in.

They all seemed to know and nodded in unison.

"And didn't the paper say the cops suspected that he was behind that thing last night."

"No," the woman added. "They didn't say for sure only that they thought it was mob related."

"Still you don't suppose that those two in the deli were the ones they were looking for do you."

"I doubt it," the waiter chimed in as he came to take their order. "Everyone knows that there are only three mobsters in this town that leave a calling card like that at the pawnshop."

The three in the booth waited for him to answer but having realized he may have said too much only asked for their order.

"You look pretty real for being outta town?" Patrick said as he asked him if he wanted another.

"Don't want to get too tight before dark," Dawson answered shaking his head and asked him how much he owed for the drinks.

When he told him he tossed him the money with a one hundred percent tip. As it landed on the bar he told him that he should put the extra towards keeping himself out of the can. Patrick laughed and nodded his head as he pocketed the extra.

Dawson took two steps before turning back around.

"You have any idea what that waiter was talking about," he asked.

Patrick looked around the bar before waving him closer.

"Yeah," he said in very low voice. "There are three guys that Joey knows from back in the day, if you know what I mean."

Dawson nodded knowing exactly what he meant.

"Well," he began again. "They been around town for a while now shooting up the streets Chicago style right down to the typewriters they use. Joey uses the three of them to shake things up, businesses mostly. Maybe you know them maybe you don't the three of them grew up together. They say they do everything together, but who knows for sure. Anyway they go by Stitch, Shifty, and Two Time."

"Can you do any better than that?"

Patrick said he was sorry and told him their full names. Dawson thanked him by giving him a fin.

"Strictly for that baby girl of yours."

He recognized the name Eddie Haggerty from a case in Texas when he was still a Marshal. Only they didn't call him Two Time so he couldn't be sure if it was the same one. Wasting no time he left bar and hailed a cab.

Jumping in the first cab he gave him his home address and sat back in the seat. Fishing out his cigarettes he put one between his lips and tried to sort out a few of the events of the last twenty four hours. There wasn't enough to make too many connections with Mack getting shot. As he thought about it he realized that he had forgotten to ask Abrams about the slugs they had taken out of him. That could be the difference in making the case or really twisting things up.

The cab went a block before it was stuck in traffic. The cabbie turned and apologized to him and asked him if he wanted to get out. He told the driver that the whole reason he had hailed a cab in the first place was so that he could Think and have a quick rest. Chuckling, the driver told him that he was the boss and whatever he wanted was okay with him.

Just as he closed his eyes he heard the cab door open.

"Hello Dawson," Tiny said as he got in.

The cabbie began to protest for him but Dawson said it was alright. However he was more than a little perturbed that the reporter would jump in his cab. Not to mention talk to him after trying to frame him for murder.

"If he gets to be too much of a problem I'll just shoot him and push him out the door when we take off. That is if we ever move again." Dawson said turning toward him being careful not to make his guns inaccessible. "What can I do for you Tiny?"

"Jeez," Tiny said his eyes wide with surprise. "You wouldn't really shoot me would you?"

"Don't tempt me."

"You gotta understand Dawson it wasn't my idea to hang that on you."

"You know that's the same thing your editor and publisher said when I had a talk with them."

"Okay, maybe it was my idea," he said sounding less than humble. "You gotta admit though things sure broke on that case once I did."

"Yeah they about broke my neck on the gallows thanks to you."

"Okay I admitted it," Tiny said. "And I'm sorry. Can't we just let it be water under the bridge and move on?"

"You can move on if you want," Dawson began as he reached for his gun, "right back out that door."

"Stop kidding around," Tiny laughed nervously. "I just have a few questions about what happened this afternoon at the deli."

"Are you sure I was even there?"

"I saw you leaving when I arrived."

"They make a good pastrami sandwich," Dawson laughed. "Abraham has the best pastrami in town and his coffee. Well his coffee is the best, especially when you add a little spirit of the Irish."

"Have it your way but you can't deny you were at the pawnshop last night after the shooting there."

"Pawnshop, pawnshop hmmm was I at a pawnshop last night."

"Come on Dawson gimme a break," Tiny pleaded with him.

"You know I just may have been in a pawnshop last night," he added. "Now that you mention it I was, yeah. I can't really tell you what I was doing there you know confidentiality and all that. I wouldn't want any of the women in my life to know what I was doing."

"Dammit Dawson," he complained. "How am I supposed to do my job if you refuse to answer questions?"

"Why don't you make it up like you did last time? Now if you'll excuse me," he opened the cab door and stepped out.

"Come on Dawson," Tiny protested again.

"The intruder will pay the meter," he said leaning into the driver's window, keeping an eye on Tiny.

Dawson, unnoticed by Tiny as he was beginning to complain about paying the meter, slipped the cabbie a fin. Nodding the cabbie turned his head to look at his new passenger.

"You want to pay up now or is there somewhere you want to go?"

"I'm not paying the meter," he protested.

"Look mac you pay the meter or I take you straight to the cops."

As Tiny went to get out the traffic cleared and the cab took off around the corner. Dawson stood on the sidewalk and laughed as the cab disappeared in traffic.

When he reached his apartment he went straight to the phone. He dialed Abrams' number at the station.

"Abrams," said the voice on the phone after the third ring.

"Good you're there," he returned. "What can you tell me about three guys named Stitch, Shifty, and Two Time?"

"Not an awful lot really," Abrams began. "Three hood rats is about all they are. That was their calling card last night. We've been looking for them ever since."

"Any luck yet?"

"Not that I have been told about. They run to ground pretty good after one of these things. They don't get out much that we can tell between jobs either. We haul them in every once in a while. The only trouble is there alibis are always solid. And that as you know don't do us any good at convicting them for anything."

Dawson nodded as he listened. Pouring a drink and lighting a cigarette he waited for Abrams to finish.

"Yeah, it's hard to lock someone up when enough people say they were somewhere else." He took a drag off his cigarette and sipped his whisky before asking his next question. "Do you know the caliber the slugs they took out of Mack?"

"We just figured they were forty-fives like the rest of the bullets that hit the shop. You on to something?"

"I don't know; it just doesn't make much sense is all. Let me know when you find out what they were."

Abrams said he would and he could hear him telling one of the uniforms to check it out.

"One more thing Abrams, in all the confusion and cloudiness of my brain today I forgot to ask you if he was going to be alright."

"According to the docs he's going to have a rough time of it, but he should be fine. Are you going to talk to him?"

Dawson told him he probably would and was thinking of going over after he'd had something to eat. He said his good-byes and hung up as someone began knocking on his door.

"Tiny if that's you on the other side of that door I'm just going to let my automatics answer."

"Um, Mr. Dawson," the voice sounded a little scared. "It's me Maria Leonard. You told me to come by today."

"So I did," he had forgotten.

"Come in," he said opening the door and stepping aside.

As she walked past him he apologized for threating to shoot her. He also couldn't help but smell her rose scented perfume.

"Can I get you a drink?"

She accepted and he poured her one.

"You said something about wanting to find your sister if I remember correctly."

"Yes," she returned "I don't have much money so I am afraid that if you ask too much then I will not be able to have you look for her."

"Do you have a photograph of her?" he asked hopefully.

She shook her head telling him that she knew it was probably going to be impossible. However he continued to ask questions on the off chance that the missing girl just happened to fall into his lap.

"I have to tell you," he began when she finished. "The chances on finding your sister after almost elven years and not having seen her since she was fourteen are fairly slim. Even with a photograph it could be near impossible. Now maybe if you knew the name of the man she went away with I might have some place to start."

"I know it's probably a lost cause Mr. Dawson," she said lowering her head. "Anyway I … well I just can't let myself give up that's all."

"I know a few places I can ask around, but like I said I'm not going to make any promises."

"How much you gonna charge me?" she asked looking a little more hopeful again. "I don't have much but if you're willing to let me work something out with you."

She reached out and touched his arm as she talked. Giving him an idea of the ways she might be willing to work something out with him. He couldn't say it wasn't a tempting offer, but he was fairly sure that it would only complicate things later on. Besides he wasn't sure there even was a sister. It was something he would have to figure out over dinner. They finished their drinks and he offered to take her for dinner. She seemed disappointed, but accepted his offer just the same. After pointing to a bathroom where she could freshen up he went to change into his dinner clothes. Thanking him she disappeared behind the door.

As they were ready to leave the phone rang.

"Dawson," Abrams said half out of breath as he answered.

"You sound like you just took on the Boston marathon."

"Mike 'The Nose' just tried to escape the hospital," he returned his breath slowly returning to normal. "I just had to run him down. Listen I got the bullets from the Doctors."

"The ones they took out of the Pawnbroker?"

"Yeah I had them sent to the crime boys."

"They weren't forty-five's were they?"

"No they weren't, but how did you know? You aren't holding out on me are you?"

"You wouldn't be calling me half out of breath if they had been." He smiled a little as he remembered what Mack had told him. "Listen I think I'll take a look around the pawnshop tomorrow. You wanna come with me?"

"I'll have to get back to you on that," he returned finally catching his breath. "You on your way out?"

"Yeah," he said lighting cigarette. "There's a songbird here that says she's hungry."

On the other end of the phone Abrams shook his head as he called him a lucky man.

"People got to eat," Dawson returned smiling at his waiting dinner guest.

Hanging up the phone he offered his elbow to the singer.

It was close to four in the afternoon by the time Carolyn and Douglas returned from their horse ride. Barnes was happy enough just being close to her but he couldn't allow himself to get too comfortable with her again. At least not until he found out what it was that made her leave two years earlier. He could tell that she wasn't ready to tell him. Not wanting to push the issue he decided that he would wait until she was.

"I thought maybe we would stay in tonight," he said as they walked into the house. "I've invited a few of our friends over for dinner if that's alright with you."

"Sure darling whatever you say," she returned. "It'll be nice to see some of them again."

Up in her room she took a shower and started to dress. She hadn't thought about the night before all day. However sitting there alone there was nothing to keep her mind from going there.

Tears began streaming over her cheeks as she thought of Pop laying on the floor bleeding. If only she had stopped to see him earlier they might not have gotten him. Then again, she thought, she might have been lying on the floor next to him. She cursed Joey and his boys. Maybe Pop had been right, maybe Dawson was her only hope. She'd met him once at a dinner party that Douglas had held for members of his law firm. Still she didn't know enough about him to trust him with her life. In her mind her only choice was to keep hiding. What was it that her Uncle used to tell her? 'The best place to hide was in plain sight,' something like that anyway. There were too many questions and not enough answers. Maybe she should have stopped and talked to Dawson like she had planned. She'd sent him the note asking him to be there but then rain had ruined it. It was the rain that kept them from having the welcome home party out on the street like they planned. That's why she wanted to meet him there in public. That way they would be just part of the crowd and she could continue hiding. She was used to it, in a way she'd been hiding since she was fourteen. She thought for a minute of the many names she had used over the years. If she had to be honest she wasn't even sure if she even remembered her real name. That realization only made her cry harder. She was sure that Douglas had no idea what she'd been when she met him. As far as she was concerned that life ended that night when she told him her name was Carolyn. She laughed as she realized that she couldn't think of the name she'd been using the second before she met him. Wiping her tears she put on her best face and finished dressing.

Most of the dinner guests had arrived and the drinks were flowing freely by the time she went downstairs. There were more than she had expected to see on such short notice. Then again an invitation to the Douglas Barnes home for anything commanded a lot of attention. Even if he was no longer one of the city's leading Attorneys, he was still a member of one of its most respected families.

"Oh there you are darling," a woman called as she came down the stairs.

All eyes in the room turned and watched as she descended the last few steps on the grand staircase.

"It's so good to see you Mrs. Summers," Carolyn returned taking the woman's hand when she reached the bottom step. "And you as well Mrs. Parker."

Jamie floated by with a tray of drinks; grabbing one she let Mrs. Summers lead her around the crowd of people. She remembered them all as she looked around. Nearly all of their old friends were there. Along with the Summers and Parkers there were the Mr. and Mrs. Millers, Fosters, Cards, Johnsons, and Handlers, as well as the widow Cynthia Chamberlin and her companion Miss Dora Winters. Douglas never missed anything she mused; he'd even managed to find a singer and piano player. She couldn't be sure, but she thought that she even recognized them.

"You know dear when Douglas called we were all set to leave for the Parkers," she said as she led her around. "So naturally we had to turn him down. Wouldn't you know it when we arrived to the Parkers they had decided to come over here so here we are the bunch of us. There was no way really that we could have turned down poor Douglas, at least that is what we agreed on when we all arrived at the Parkers."

Carolyn finished her drink in three gulps as she tried hard to be polite and not bolt back up the stairs. Noticing her plight Jamie made her way back toward her.

"Oh, Dorothy I'm sure Carolyn doesn't need to know all of that," Mrs. Althea Parker, said kissing Carolyn on the cheek. "All she needs to know is that Douglas told us that she was here and that we dropped everything and came to see her."

"Dinners at our house are so boring," her husband, Albert

added. "Besides Douglas has better hooch."

There was a brief 'here, here' in the background as the other guests agreed with his observation. After a few minutes the group of dinner guests gathered around raising their glasses in unison as they each offered up a toast in her honor. The cocktail hour was actually two before dinner was served. She did her best to dodge many of the questions they asked her, but she couldn't dodge them all. She laughed off most of the questions or just simply gave vague answers. When they were all seated for dinner she finally answered the one that was on all their minds and had asked most often.

"I know you all want to know what happened," she began standing up a bit unsteadily. "Well, I'll tell you what happened. I went away to south Florida so that I could have Douglas' illegitimate baby."

The room was silent and filled with shocked faces as she paused for affect. Even Douglas' face had turned white.

"And," she began again when she had felt that she had achieved the desired effect. "I want you to be the first to meet her. There she is now."

Pointing to Jamie, the maid, she asked her to take a bow. The young girl wasn't sure what she should do, but she managed a half bow half curtsey before turning red and running out of the room. The dinner guests laughed finally and nothing more was asked about her absence that night. At least they didn't ask her again. However, they did continue to speculate among themselves. Being the good hostess, she was sure to spend at least a few minutes with each one of her guests over the course of the evening. Ever the vigilant server Jamie made sure that she had a fresh drink each time she moved to a new guest.

Admittedly after dinner the night became a bit of a blur for her that is until their guests were leaving and they had an unexpected visitor.

Joey 'Tuna' Fisher pushed his way into the house giving Harold a shove and knocking him to the floor.

"Well ain't this just cozy," he said as he confronted the guests. "All this for me? Here all I wanted to do was to come by and say hello. If I'd a known you'se were going to have a party I woulda come by sooner."

Two of his goon's came through the door behind him. Both carried a Thompson and an automatic in a shoulder holster. Neither of them wore a jacket making the weapons appear more menacing and easier to get to.

"Normally," he began again. "At this point I would have you hand over all your money and jewelry. Only I'm in a good mood today, well there was that thing earlier when the cops killed one of my best boys and wounded another. That cost me a few thousand clams so I really should be in a bad mood. However, it looks like I just found my girl again. In which case I think I can let you all go without taking the time to relieve you of the weight of all those things. Now scram!"

Joey walked over and took the drunken girl into his arms and gave her kiss on the lips. When he finished she slapped him twice across the face. He laughed at her and threw her across the room. She'd bloodied his lip and still laughing he licked the blood away.

"I think that you and I have some business to take care of," he said taking Barnes by the back of his shirt. "Why don't we go someplace a bit less crowded?"

"Everything will be alright," Barnes told them all as he offered no resistance.

"You should have stayed back in the neighborhood." Joey said walking past Carolyn as she was being helped up by Albert Parker. "Things would have gone better for lover boy here."

Barnes pointed the way to the library and the two went in closing the door behind them. Carolyn knew exactly what was being said. There was no doubt that Joey was telling him all about her past. She doubted he would leave anything out, not even the year that she had been his mistress.

Mickey appeared in the door behind Joeys two goons; his large frame filling the door.

"It's okay Mickey," Harold whispered. "The Mister is taking care of things. I don't think he wants anything to happen, at least not here or now."

Mickey nodded and disappeared back into the night before either of the goons saw him. There would be another time. He was sure of that and then there would be no problems with who might see him.

Joey came out of the library about ten minutes later. Smiling he tipped his hat and made his way to the door.

"You'se got a right good gentleman there honey," he said looking directly at Carolyn. "I think he and I are going to be great friends after all."

The three uninvited guests left almost as abruptly as they came. The dinner guests, who hadn't dared move or leave the house, now poured over Carolyn telling her how brave she had been to slap the gangsters face. None however dared to ask her how he knew her or why he had kissed her. It did help to fuel even more speculation as to what had happened in the past two years.

Snapping back into her role of hostess again she saw their guests to the door. After everyone had left Harold quietly went into the library. He came out after a quick minute disappearing into the kitchen. She knew when Douglas hadn't come out of the library that he would probably never look at her the same way again.

Mickey stood by each of the guest's cars as they pulled up to make sure nothing would happen as they left. When they were all in their cars he opened the main gate letting them leave. As for the uninvited guests, Mickey made a promise to himself that they would never get onto the grounds again. After closing the gate behind the dinner guests he went to the doors that led into library and looked in on his boss.

Sitting slumped in his chair behind the large desk Douglas Barnes had a look on his face that said his whole world had collapsed, again. He heard his chauffeur tapping on the glass doors. Looking up he shook his head briefly and waved his hand palm down towards the door. Satisfied that at least his boss was alive the big man turned and went back to the carriage house. Knowing that if he was needed that would be where he would look for him first. Cook came out a short time later and filled him in on everything that happened in the house that he had missed.

Carolyn stood in the middle of the foyer outside of the library and stared at the door hoping that he would at least come out and talk to her. At least let her explain her side of what she knew Joey had told him. However he didn't come out. She tried to get in only to find that the door was locked. Pushing against it she called out begging to be let in. After a few minutes she slid down the front of the door, crying. Jamie tried several times to help her up, but it was useless, after a few minutes she gave up. A minute later Carolyn had cried herself to sleep where she lay.

Douglas didn't want to hear what he'd been told. In his eyes she couldn't be any of the things he'd said she'd been. Although when it was all said and done he knew two things for sure. He wasn't about to let Joey bleed him and he never wanted to lose her again. Her past was always something that he didn't care about, at least until then. There was nothing he could do to change it. Just the same, he couldn't look at her after Joey had left. After she passed out he got Mickey to carry her upstairs and Jamie to put her to bed. It wasn't his proudest moment, but it was the best he could do at the time.

All he could think of now was to find out just how much of it was true. There were only one or two people that he could talk to that he could trust to tell him the truth. When Mickey was finished he had him bring the car around. Within an hour after Joey had left his estate he was in the city checking the nightclubs hoping to find the latest address of at least one of those two people. On his fourth stop he happened on a bartender, Kid Pat, who he had defended on a burglary charge early in his career. A sawbuck later, and he had one of the addresses he'd wanted.

Cecelia Robbins hadn't worked a day in her life at least not since she figured out the difference between boys and girls. It was only a matter of time until she figured out what boys would do to get girls and what girls would do to get away from home. From there she never looked back. Barnes had defended her on a bootlegging and running an illegal boarding house several years earlier. Prohibition was in full swing yet she never once considered what would happen if she were convicted. She had dirt on just about every Judge on the bench at the time and enough politicians to start her own country. She threatened to spill it all if it even looked like they would give her time on the charge. It might not have been the smartest thing to do but she knew too much and was too well connected to take the chance. Needless to say she got off without so much as a slap on the wrist. Even the papers had printed a full front page retraction. He could only imagine how many of them she had dirt on now.

Her address was further uptown closer to the ritzier part of the city from the last time he'd visited. It was a five story brownstone with a wrought iron fence in front. A stoop let it sit back from the street with ten steps that led to the front door. Standing at the top of the stoop he was about to knock when it was opened by a large man in tuxedo that just barely fix.

"Welcome," the big man said bowing his head and waving his arm to the right.

Two barely dressed girls each took an arm and led him into the parlor. A smile flashed across Cecelia's face as she recognized her former lawyer.

"I'll take this one ladies," she said almost tripping over the furniture to get them away from him.

Holding back a laugh he smiled as he watched her come toward him. The years since he had seen her last hadn't been all that kind to her. She would never have been called the prettiest girl in the room; her body was considered her best feature. She had always dressed in the newest form fitting fashions. Her eyes seemed to sparkle as she spoke to you. However, it was her warm and inviting smile that made her so good at her job. That was the last time he'd seen her. Today her smile showed a few missing teeth, her eyes looked dull and lifeless. Her clothes were more than a couple of years out of style, and were too big for her.

"I didn't think you would ever have need of my services," she told him as she took his hand and steered him to her office.

They stopped only long enough to grab a bottle and two glasses from the small bar in the corner of the foyer. Her office was messy, newspapers and letters covered her desk. Pouring a drink she finally asked him why he was there. He hesitated for a minute not sure how to begin. He even found himself reverting to a moment of flattering her to charm her, although he didn't know why. Eventually he worked up the courage to ask her the questions that he wanted the answers to. It wasn't until he told her that she might have been with Joey a year earlier that she recognized who he was talking about.

"To be one hundred proof positive I would need to see a photograph," She smiled pouring out a tall glass. "Until then I might be wrong. Although, your Carolyn does sound like a girl that worked for me a few years back. From what I hear she ain't in the business no more, left me flat. You say you've known her for about four years?"

Barnes nodded not quite sure what to say, his heart still sinking as she spoke.

"Yeah I would say that's about right. Only when she worked for me she used a different name, lots of different names actually. She liked to use different names, seems to me that she'd change her name once a week sometimes. I know that she'd use a different name for every house she worked in. I think she sometimes used two or three different ones at the same time. For all I know it excites her, you know. To each his own for all I care. As long as I get my cut I don't care what they like to do right."

She was laughing hard as she finished talking, before long she was coughing.

He felt as if he was being stabbed as she spoke, but then again he'd always suspected there was a lot more that she had never told him about. For instance, the coat she'd been wearing the night they'd met certainly wasn't one that an ordinary seamstress could afford. Digging in his overcoat he pulled out a photograph he'd taken of Carolyn a week after they'd met and showed it to her.

"That's her alright," she said finishing her drink and pouring another. "Yeah, she went by Sarah, Jennifer, Margaret, Betty, too many names really for me to keep track of. She was a good girl though, never had no trouble with her. Kept her nose clean if you know what I mean. Drank a little too much from time to time but never had no problems. She came to me when she was just a little bit of a thing. Loved her as if she were one of my own I did, she told me she'd found herself a good man. Wished I would have known it was you then. Could have solved all kinds of problems I'm sure."

He stood up and thanked her not really wanting to hear anymore.

"It's all in the timing isn't it," he laughed.

"It sure is," she returned and laughed too. "One more thing counselor; you shouldn't be too hard on her when you get home. People do things that they may not always want to do. If only to get where they think they want to go. Once they get where they're going they can't change the way they got there no matter how hard they try. And I would say that if she called you last night then that's where she really wants to be."

"Who would have thought you would have turned out to be so wise." He laughed again and left her pouring yet another drink. "You should see a doctor about that cough, it doesn't sound so good."

She told him that she had and that he was right.

Back in his car he waved to the beat cop that was across the street as they pulled away.

"I think I need a drink Mickey," he called from the back seat. "That is unless you know of anything that we can interrupt."

Nodding Mickey passed a small black bag over the seat.

It was just before three am when the Lincoln came to a stop

on the wharf. They watched for a few minutes making sure that what they were looking for was there. The chauffeur was the first out of the car pulling the mask over his face he waited for his passenger join him.

When they were ready they walked down the dock. As they reached the warehouse they were looking for, a small freighter was pulling away from in front of it. Mickey made easy work of the two men that had been left outside to keep an eye out for trouble. Quickly tying them up Barnes joked that maybe he should go out west and become a Rodeo star. Shaking his head the chauffeur picked up their typewriters and tossed them into the water. Inside the warehouse office three men were busy checking and counting the packages. While two others were busy counting and checking a satchel of cash.

Wasting little time they circled around the office and waited for them to come out. It would be easy enough they had done it all before and in the very same warehouse. It wasn't long before two of the men came out carrying the satchel of cash. Barnes nodded to Mickey; nodding back he followed the men out. The other three men were busy loading the packages into six other satchels. They were laughing as they sampled some of the packages themselves. Mickey was back a couple of minutes later and settled next to his boss.

The phone rang in the office and one of them answered. It was short conversation they couldn't hear any of it but when they hung up the three men hurriedly finished packing the satchels.

"Come on hurry up Tuna's expecting us," one of them said opening the office door.

"Was that him on the phone Smitty?" asked one of the others.

"Yeah," Smitty returned. "Who do you think it'd be this time of night, fer cryin out loud? You're not the smartest bum in your family are you?"

The second reached for his heater and cursed at him

"Knock it off you crumbs," the third interrupted pushing the two apart. "We ain't got time for this, let's get on with it."

Agreeing they would have it out at another time they each picked up two satchels and called out to let the others know they were coming out.

While they were arguing Barnes and Mickey had made their way back out of the warehouse and were waiting for them. As the three men came out Mickey grabbed the last two and knocked their heads together. The bodies of the two men went limp immediately and slumped to the ground. Barnes was behind the last man standing with both of his revolvers aimed at his chest. No words were spoken as the man noticed his two companions on the ground. Dropping the two satchels he lifted his hands up over his head. As Mickey began tying the three men together with the first two, Barnes made his way up the dock crane. When the men were securely tied they made quick work of the packages tearing each one open before tossing it into the bay. A half hour after they arrived the two were making their way back through the city streets.

"I'm a little hungry," Barnes said from the backseat.

"Usual place?" he asked.

Barnes nodded and settled back in the comfort of the back seat.

Three hours later Joey would find his men hanging ten feet off the ground, suspended from a loading crane in a cargo net. As usual none of them could describe who it was that had attacked them. Then again they didn't want to admit that there were only two of them. It was a familiar problem he'd been having over the past couple of years. Over the next few days and weeks he'd have more men at every exchange, but nothing would happen. When he'd cut back it was only a matter of time before he was hit again. As many people as he had in his pocket he still couldn't find anyone that knew anything about them. He had a few ideas of his own and for his money there was only one man that had the brass to do what they had been doing.

Dawson made it a short night, wanting a clear head the next morning. After taking the songbird to dinner he dropped her off at Mike's Place. He stayed only long enough to have a few drinks with Jimmy and Benny while listening to her sing. Leaving before he got too tight the songbird acted a little disappointed but then again she wasn't the only girl in Mike's Place that was. In spite of her best efforts the blonde coat check girl couldn't get him to stay either.

Back in his apartment he turned on the radio and sat down in an ugly large overstuffed chair in the living room. It was an ungodly looking chair, but it was comfortable to sit and sleep in. It was the only reason he kept it, that and the fact that Jane was always after him to get rid of it. Pouring a drink and lighting a cigarette he ran the last two days over in his head.

He knew that the two typists were Joey's boys trying to shake the street down for protection. Only they weren't the ones that hit the Pawnbroker. He had guessed the slugs were thirty-two's or thirty-eight's when he had seen the wounds. Then there was what he had whispered to him. It didn't really make too much sense to him but he kept it in the mix just the same hoping that he could make it all come out right. No he said finally. There was more to it than he could see just then. He needed to spend some time looking around the pawnshop and then having a long chat with Mack that is if he came to by then. However it worked out, he was sure that he or Abrams would figure it out soon enough. He spent a few hours listening to the radio, smoking cigarettes, and sipping some fine brandy before he finally fell asleep.

It was a little after three in the morning when officer Jacks made his way to the nurse's station. He'd just gotten back after being relieved by one of the orderly's so he could visit the little officer's room. Nurse Simon had waved to him as she passed him in the hall. He checked on Mr. Morre before he went to see her. On the off chance that Abrams had snuck in again while he had been gone.

"Hello handsome," she said as he stood in front of her.

She was the only one at the desk when he came up. He acknowledged her by tipping his hat. He wasn't quite sure what to say to her. He only knew that he didn't want to get in trouble with her supervisor.

"Aw, don't mind her," she began when she noticed how nervous he was. "She's an old softy. Besides she can't stop me from talkin to no one as long as I do my work."

"That's nice," he said. "Listen I been wondering, since we both get off work about the same time I was thinking that maybe you might want to go get something to eat with me or maybe have a drink or some coffee."

"Why wait?" She smiled, touching his arm.

Leaving the desk she tilted her head to get him to follow her.

Looking around he followed her down the hallway. They turned into a small linen closet just a few doors down from the nurse's station. Giggling she locked the door behind them, threw her arms around his neck and turned out the light.

At the change of shifts sometime after Officer Jacks and Nurse Simon had left. Doctor Sarah Dennison who had been at the hospital all night delivering a new life into the neighborhood stopped in to check on her father's old friend. Instead of finding what she had hoped to be a living patient she found Edward 'Pop' Morre dead in his bed. Noticing the color of his skin she immediately could tell that he had been suffocated.

He woke to the sound of knuckles wrapping hard on his front door. Dawson, still in his dinner clothes from the night before, got up from his chair and sleepily made his way to the door gripping one of his automatics. The knocking had stopped by the time he got there, but he asked who was there just the same. When no one answered he opened the door just in time to see Jane and one of her friends getting on to the elevator.

"You give up too easily," he shouted down the hallway. "That may very well be your biggest problem."

The two laughed as they saw him, his shirt fully unbuttoned

his hair disheveled and his pants beginning to fall down.

"You better check your southern exposure before you get arrested," Jane said turning around. "We've come to make you breakfast, that is if you're interested."

Dawson smiled and told them he was as he grabbed for his suspenders.

"You remember my friend Andrea don't you," Jane said as the two passed him and stepped inside his apartment.

Andrea was a gorgeous strawberry blonde with more than enough curves to keep a man interested.

"The day I forget Andrea is the day I want you to put a bullet in my brain. I am sure life won't be worth living if I can't remember such a creature."

Jane smiled but inside she had always been jealous of the way men looked and talked to her friend. It wasn't as if she didn't get her fair share of stares, but for whatever the reason none of the men she knew ever flirted with her like they did with Andrea; with the exception of Dawson. Andrea on the other hand had heard it all before, but whatever he said to her managed to sound new and not in the least bit like he was trying too hard to impress her.

"You go take a shower and get rid of the 'I was drunk last night' smell," Jane insisted shooing him away, "while we girls make you a good hearty breakfast."

"I'll have you know I was home early last night," he told her, "and I wasn't tight. That as you know is quite a feat for me."

"Then why is it that you're still dressed in your dinner clothes," she returned.

"You mean almost dressed in his dinner clothes," Andrea chuckled.

"I fell asleep in my chair listening to the radio if you must know."

"You mean she hasn't gotten rid of that big comfy chair yet," Andrea said pushing past him. "I love this chair."

She let out a long sigh as she sat in the ugly chair.

"You see darling someone gets it," he returned shaking his

thumb in her direction.

"And you both need to have your heads examined." Jane laughed as she began getting out his frying pans and turning on the stove. "Hey turn up that radio so we can hear it."

It was a morning music program and Andrea came dancing back into the kitchen.

"Dance with me darling," she said taking Jane's hand.

"You're going to make him think all sorts of things," Jane laughed and pulled away.

"Well it's nothing that might not be true darling," she teased kissing her on the cheek.

Leaning against the cabinets he smiled as he watched them dance about the kitchen. It had been a long time since he'd seen the two together. He'd almost forgotten how much he enjoyed their company. When the song ended they turned, bowed to each other and then to him as he applauded their performance. He was still smiling as he made his way to his bedroom and into his private bathroom. He was stepping into the shower when they both appeared behind him.

"You see darling," Jane said as they pushed the door open. "He really does look as good now as he did the last time we saw him."

Dawson began to protest, but he knew it was useless to do so. One at a time he might have had a chance, but not when the two of them were together.

"I just love watching a man shower," Jane added after a bit.

"Me too," Andrea echoed, "especially this one."

"Hey aren't you two supposed to be making breakfast," he called out over the sound of the shower.

"Oh we are dear," Andrea replied. "Right now we are making sure that it is properly cleaned."

"You two are incorrigible; and that's encouraging."

"Perhaps we are dear," she added. "And right now I think we'd settle for an invitation to join you."

"Now, now, mustn't do that I haven't had my breakfast yet and I am sure I will need every advantage I can get I can get for that."

"You're no fun at all," Jane said laughing as she turned to leave. "When he's done be sure that he makes it back to the kitchen as sober as he is now."

"I'm not sure what fun that will be but I will try," Andrea added giving her a slap on her bottom as she left.

Jane jumped, letting out a little yelp as the hand connected.

As he stepped out of the shower she surprised him by handing him a towel.

"I thought you had gone out with Jane."

"Nope, like I said I love to watch a man shower."

"I thought you had your own man to watch take a shower?"

"Eh, he was way too jealous," she said helping him towel off. "I had to get rid of him. It was a terrible break up. He wouldn't leave me alone for weeks. Thankfully Jane was there to discourage him from doing anything stupid."

He couldn't say that he didn't enjoy the pampering but he was still nervous as to what Jane would have to say about it when they were alone.

"Whatever happened to your butler and cook?" she asked out of nowhere, changing the subject. "Did you have to let them go, did they steal from you, or are you low on funds?"

"I retired them before I went out of town a while back." He said as she helped him put his robe on. "I haven't had the heart to replace them yet. I have a cleaning service that works with the building come in everyday to keep the place tidy."

"I think you need to get married and let your wife take care of the house."

"Is that an offer?" he asked turning to face her.

He grabbed her shoulders and kissed her nose before she could answer.

"Well, I, uh, maybe, why not? You could do worse," she returned nervously looking him in the eyes.

"I couldn't do any better either I'm sure." He kissed her again this time on her forehead.

She was confused, relieved and happy at his words as she

followed him to his room like a little puppy. She sat on the edge of the bed and watched him. She couldn't help but think of how it might feel to be able to do it every morning. She sighed softly as he dropped his robe on the bed and began to dress. For his own part he did his best to not think about or look at the beautiful woman that was sitting on his bed watching his every move.

"That a new scar?" she asked pointing to a pinkish red mark on his right side.

"Hmm, oh yeah I got that a little while back." He rubbed his finger over it as he talked. "Don't tell Jane she'll want a full account of it and then me. I won't be able to get dressed again until midnight."

"Mmmm now that sounds like it could be heavenly," she smiled as she looked up.

He couldn't help but notice the sparkle in her gray eyes as she talked. All sorts of ideas began running though his mind as he looked at her. Just the same he finished dressing and offered her his arm.

"There you are," Jane began as they entered the kitchen, "I was just about to send out search party."

"And we were close to having to send up a signal flare," Andrea laughed.

As they ate breakfast the two women talked about clothes, shopping, and whatever gossip they had heard since the last time they'd seen each other. He liked the sound of their voices and was content listening to them. It was going to be a good day. When they had finished, it was Andrea that took it on herself to wash the dishes. He kept telling her not to worry about it as the service would take care of it after he left for the day. When the phone rang a few minutes later Jane picked it up as if it were her own.

"Dawson residence," she said smacking her lips while she listened as if she were chewing gum. "Yeah, he's here just a moment."

She turned her head giggling as she handed him the

receiver.

"This is me," he said taking it from her.

He listened as Abrams told him that Mack was dead.

"Docs think he was smothered," he continued. "That dumbass Jacks is going to be pounding a beat for a very long time."

"You sure he didn't do it?" he asked immediately returning to his cynical self.

"Positive," he returned disgusted with himself and the officer. "It seems he and one of the night nurses locked themselves in one of the linen closets and where playing Doctor."

"Are you sure about the time?"

"Very sure, one of the Nurses on duty noticed that he wasn't at the door. According to her she went into Morre's room looking for Jacks but she couldn't find him. Pop was alive when she checked in on him then, so she called down to get an orderly to come up to the floor to watch the room. He hadn't shown up yet by the time she had to leave the desk for an emergency in one of the other rooms. Any way just after shift change Doc Dennison, you remember, the red head from yesterday went into his room and found him dead. They're all trying to say that they had looked in on him. Each one saying they didn't notice anything out of place so none of them went in for a closer look. I don't believe a word of it though I don't think any of them checked."

Dawson shook his head as he listened and debated on whether or not he should tell him what Morre had said the night he was shot. He wasn't sure if he was right in his decision, but he still wanted a chance to chase that lead on his own.

"Did you find anything out anything more about the slugs?"

"They're thirty-eights according to the lab boys."

"Well that narrows it down a little."

"To every cop and two-bit hood on the street," he returned. "Sure narrows it down alright."

"I imagine you're going to be there for a while yet."

"A lot longer than I wanted to be I can tell you that. I'll catch up with you later and we can go over to the pawnshop."

As he hung up the phone he asked the women what they had planned for the day.

"We thought we'd stick close to you," Jane began. "Maybe take you out to lunch."

"Then letting us entertain you with a little afternoon dress shopping," Andrea added. "Then you could buy us dinner and from there whatever happens, well happens."

"I'm going to have to pass on part of that," he said taking each one in an arm. "You girls can stay here as long as you want. I can meet you back here when I'm done."

"We'll go with you then," Jane insisted.

"Yeah," Andrea chimed in. "I'll bet we'll make great gumshoe assistants or whatever it is that you call them."

"No, I don't think …" he began to protest but somehow knew it was going to be a losing battle.

"Please," the two women said in unison batting their eyes at him.

"Alright," he said after a bit more pleading on their part. "Only you must do everything I say when I say it and not one second of questions when I tell you."

The two came to attention gave him a salute and said yes sir with a serious but mocking look on their faces. Breaking the salute they held out his shoulder holsters and waited for him.

"Dear Lord what have I gotten myself into," he chuckled as he slipped the pro-offered holsters over his shoulders.

As they strapped it to him he took his time checking his guns making sure they were fully loaded and that he had a couple of extra magazines for each one. When they finished Andrea went to her hand bag and took out her own thirty-two automatic, checked it and her spare ammo. Lifting her dress she strapped it and its holster to the top of her stocking on her right leg. Jane and Dawson both raised their eyebrows as they watched her. His mind wandered back to their conversation earlier as she pulled out its twin and called Jane over to her. Yup, he thought again, he probably couldn't do much better. She protested at first but Andrea kept insisting and finally she gave in. Strapping the gun to Jane's left thigh she told her not to worry that the safety was and that it was only for just in case anyway.

"That's what worries me," Jane said when she'd finished.

It felt strange and cold against her thigh as she walked around the apartment trying to get used to its weight. If she had she taken the time to think she would have run at the sight of it.

In all honesty she had only wanted to go because Andrea wanted to. By the time the gun had a chance to warm up she too began to warm up to the idea of going along to help. Besides she thought, it just might be the idea that finally breaks her case with him. Grabbing their hats and overcoats they left his apartment.

When she woke up she was in her bed and had no idea how she had gotten there or who had undressed her. She never liked the feeling of falling asleep in one place and waking in another until she had met him. Although after remembering everything that had happened the night before she couldn't be sure if he had been the one to put her there or not. Rolling over she buried her face in the pillows and began to cry all over again. Her life was ruined, she had already known that. To have him know everything probably meant her hope that one day she would be able to make amends with him was lost. A few minutes later Jamie made her way into the room greeting her cheerily she set about as she did every morning. Opening curtains picking up the scattered clothes to be cleaned, and in general helping to do what needed to be done.

"Is Douglas awake?" she asked her.

"The Mister? Yes Miss Carolyn, he sure is."

"Where is he? I want to talk to him."

"I can't say fo'sur."

"Is he in the house?"

"No Miss," Jamie returned. "He taked off out da house afta Mickey brung you to up here so's I can put ya ta bed."

She thanked her as she left her alone again. Showering and

dressing quickly she picked up the phone and asked the operator for a number.

"It's me Irina," she said into the phone when they answered. "Irina York."

Irina York was the name they had picked to use if ever either of them ever needed the other one.

She listened for a second.

"Yeah I know," she added, "listen can I come over?"

She listened again.

"I know," she began to plead, "but I need to talk to you."

Listening again she waited for her answer.

"Okay, I'll get there as soon as I can," she added hanging up.

Looking around the room she made sure that she didn't leave anything behind. That part was easy especially since she hadn't brought anything with her except her shoulder bag. She knew that there was no way that she could get out of the house without being seen. Instead of trying she called the stables and had them get her horse ready. Calling down to the kitchen she asked Cook to make her up a basket to take with her. Changing into something more appropriate for riding she tucked her dress into her shoulder bag. Once she was downstairs she hid it in the basket that cook had made up.

Making her way to the edge of the property closest to town she led the horse to a small patch of grass and let him go. Walking to the road she changed quickly leaving her riding clothes behind. There was a chance that she would run into him on the road but it was one that she had to take. Carrying the picnic basket and sticking out her thumb she turned her back, for the second time, on the life that she had always wanted.

The road wasn't very busy so she had to walk a little ways, but soon enough a car slowed down taking a long look at her. Thankfully he was hurried along by a truck behind him.

"You need a ride honey?" asked the woman sticking her head out from the passenger side of the truck as it stopped.

She told her that she did.

"If you don't mind sitting with sacks of potatoes you can climb up there in back with my boys." She pointed her thumb to the back of the truck. "We're goin into the city so if's you wanna stop somewhere before there you just let me know now."

She told her that wherever they were stopping in the city would be just fine. Not one of the four dirty faced boys were much older than eight or nine but they all helped her as she climbed on the truck.

Forty five minutes later they were in the city. Five minutes later, after giving her thanks and adding her picnic basket to their food for the day Sally Masters sat in the back of a taxi as it cruised through the city streets.

She tried not to think about anything that had happened in the last forty eight hours but it was too hard. She couldn't get two images out of her mind. One of them was Pop lying on the floor of his pawnshop and the other was the way Douglas looked at her as he and Joey went into the library.

"Hey, Lady," the cabbie hollered grumpily from the front seat. "We're there."

"Oh, sorry," she returned.

Looking at the meter she paid him giving him a little extra but not too much extra so that he would remember her. She got out of the cab and made her way into the alley. Walking three blocks she finally reached the building she was looking for. Three floors stood between her and her destination when she spotted Riley. He was standing in front of the newsstand on the corner talking to a couple of men. They looked familiar to her but from that distance she couldn't be sure. Ducking into another alley she couldn't be sure if he'd seen her or not, but she didn't want to take that chance. Finding a phone in a nearby drug store she called the same number she had earlier.

"I'm at the drugstore," she told them when they asked.

"No I can't," she returned after a few seconds. "I might be spotted by someone I don't want to see me."

Looking around she listened nervously.

"No I don't think they saw me yet."

She listened again as she glanced over her shoulder at the door.

"Okay," she said finally and hung up.

Waiting she took her time and walked through the drug store looking at the merchandise as she made her toward the back.

"You Irina?" asked the teen coming up to her after several minutes.

She said she was. He told her to follow him as he led her into the back of the store. They made their way past stacks of boxes and discarded items. When they came to a large wooden crate he kicked the bottom of it and gave it shove. There was a soft click as it pushed back and away from the wall. He pulled the crate toward him revealing a doorway. Taking her hand he led her through it, pulling the crate closed behind them. As the crate clicked closed a door clicked open at the other end.

"Prohibition," he said as he pushed the door open to reveal a stairway.

She smiled at him as he led her down the stairs by her hand.

"Just keep following the wall straight ahead," he told her letting go of her hand when they reached the bottom. "Don't go into any of the rooms or you might get lost down here."

"But what about," she began to ask.

"They'll be at the other end." He called back from the top of the stairs. "Remember just follow the wall and don't go into any of the rooms."

The hall was fairly well lit with some natural light coming from glass cobble stones that were in the sidewalk and alley. She'd walked about half a block when she saw her friend standing near an open door.

The two women hugged as they met. When they finally let go of each other they both had tears in their eyes. Laughing they wiped them off each other's cheeks.

"Come on you can hide out at my place," Karen, her friend told her. "You need a job?"

She had known Karen Page since she was fourteen. They both had Cecelia Robbins in common. Karen was a couple of years older but still they bonded from the first day they'd met.

"That depends," she replied.

"Nah," her friend answered before she even asked. "All you have to do is answer the phone, take messages and make a few appointments."

"So it's on the level?"

"Eh," Karen laughed as she wiggled her hands.

"I'm gonna need a place to stay for a while too, if it's alright."

"Sure so long as you don't mind livin' down here." Karen took her hand and led her a few hundred feet further down the hallway.

"Let me show you the layout," she said opening the door they had come to.

Inside the room were four switchboards. There were a couple of girls sitting at two of them that Sally thought she recognized from the old days.

"We work primarily at night and on weekends," she said sitting at an open switchboard. "We answer for doctors, lawyers and whoever else. We got a bunch of the girls from the old days too, we set appointments for them they all pay a set rate each month. I keep it down here because I didn't want to lose any rent from any of the apartments. I'll get one of the girls to show you how to work this thing later. Come on I'll show where you can hide out."

Karen had been given the building a few years earlier in a will. The family had done everything they could to get it away from her. In the end after a short court battle the Judge ruled in her favor. There were a few rumors that Cecelia had a hand in the final ruling. How ever it had happened in the end she ended up with it free and clear.

The two went through another door and up another short hallway.

"We're in my building now," she told her. "I always like hearing that, my building, it's all mine."

The two laughed as she said it over again.

"This is the way out of the tombs," she told her when they

came to a stairway. There is also a door to the street from the apartment."

Unlocking the door at the bottom of the stairs she told her it was hers if she wanted it.

"It isn't the penthouse," she told her as she showed her everything. "But it's got everything you could need. If you want it I can take the rent from your pay. That is if you want the job too."

She told her that she would take both. Not that she really needed a job. The money from the jewelry she'd been selling off was enough to keep her for a while just as long as she didn't get too extravagant.

"Do I dare ask what name you're going by these days?"

Sally shook her head, and told her that she'd be changing it anyway so it really didn't matter.

"Although I always liked the name Abbey," she added "I might as well start using that one. I'll have to remember to think of a last name later. "

"Okay Abbey," Karen laughed. "You might as well know now, I'm still Karen, I haven't changed one bit. I still drink too much, and I do what I want, who I want, when I want. Before you ask, I don't care who knows it."

Sally, now calling herself Abbey, smiled as she remembered some of the things that the two of them had done. They sat at the small kitchen table and talked for a while. Karen caught her up on all the girls that they used to run around with. It was around eleven when the two went up to Karen's fourth floor apartment. There were four apartments on each of the three lower floors, while the top floor had been turned into one large apartment.

"I knew you'd like it," Karen said when she noticed Abbey's expression. I would have you up here but you said you needed a place to hide. I have too many parties for anyone to hide up here. Now if you want to do a little of the old work, then Abbey would certainly be welcome up here anytime."

"No, I think the basement is the best place for now." Abbey

returned.

Brunch was served by a young girl who couldn't have been much older than they were when they had first met. As they ate Karen told her that she knew a couple of guys that could help her move her things into the basement.

"Don't worry they can keep their mouth shut." She told her. "I use them here when I have parties, which is daily. There are some pretty important people that come and they never say anything they ain't supposed to. Besides they get paid to not remember what happens in this building."

Abbey could imagine what they were paid to not remember and she chuckled at the thought. After they ate she borrowed a hat and an overcoat. In her new disguise she made her way slowly back to the neighborhood where she had been staying, being careful not to attract too much attention. Keeping to the alleys it wasn't long before she was looking at the boarded up storefront of the pawnshop. As she slipped into the alley behind her building she saw Riley at the other end, talking to another cop.

She wanted to run but she was afraid that he would be able hear her heels as they echoed in the narrow alley. She kicked off her shoes and waited for just the right time. As he turned his back she told herself that it was now or never. Keeping her composure she made her way as if she hadn't a care in the world. She managed to open the heavy door and slip inside the building without too much difficulty. Stopping behind the closed door she gave a sigh of relief and took a deep breath. Her chest hurt and she felt as if she hadn't breathed since leaving Karen's apartment.

The air in her room smelled stale and dusty, but she didn't dare open a window. If Joey could find out where she was last night it was only a matter of time before he would know where she had been living. Being there was risky enough, she knew that, but she needed to get some things that couldn't be trusted with anyone else. When she had everything that she'd come for in her bag she knocked on the building manager's door. When there was no answer she wrote a note on an old envelope. Slipping it under the door when it was finished, she went back out the one she came in and into the alley. Immediately ducking behind a row of trash cans she looked around for Riley. She was about to leave when she saw three people come into that alley and go straight to the pawnshop. Reaching into her shoulder bag she checked to make sure that her pistol was still there. She was about to go see who it was when she spotted Riley at the other end of the alley.

Once in the street Dawson decided to walk the few blocks to the pawnshop. Jane complained about not having worn the proper shoes for all the walking they were doing. Andrea promised to make it up to her later on with a foot massage. When they reached the pawnshop he sent the girls around the corner to the newsstand for cigarettes.

"Then tell me how many steps it is from there to here," he said pointing to the door.

Jane didn't see the sense of it and with her feet hurting already she was in no mood to play. However, Andrea pulled her friend along telling her that it was all part of the fun. Meanwhile Dawson walked in front of the buildings that had been hit by bullets counting holes and steps as he went. He stood in front of the barber shop looking toward the alley running the events over in his head as did.

"You're that guy," the barber said stepping outside, "Dawson right?"

He nodded and took his outstretched hand.

"You working on finding who shot up our street?"

"Not really," he returned. "Every business owner in the city knows who shot up your street."

"Yeah," the barber smiled, "I suppose you're right."

He was around thirty-five and stood about five foot seven black hair and hazel eyes. His fingers were scarred and one of them was a little deformed.

"I'm Steve by the way," he added lighting up a cigarette and

89

offering one to Dawson.

"Good to meet you," he returned taking the cigarette. "Everyone calls me Dawson."

"They call me Stosh or just 'the barber', but mostly Stosh my family came from Prussia so I guess it's that whole Russian Pollack thing that I have going on, beats me really."

"I guess it don't matter much in this neighborhood."

"Not really, we're pretty much a mixed bag around here. Always has been as far as I know," Steve exhaled and tossed his cigarette toward the gutter. "I smoke too much, I been thinking I should quit."

"You know what they say about quitters," Dawson added shaking his head.

"Yeah," the barber returned with a chuckle, "how about a haircut?"

"Eh, why not I got nothing better to do," Dawson laughed as he saw the girls coming back around the corner.

He didn't know if they could see him but he pointed to the barber pole and followed the barber inside.

"You have this shop here long?" he asked as he got ready to cut his hair.

"My Poppa moved it here from across the street," he said combing Dawson's hair. "The building was almost brand new then. My Grand Poppa opened across the street shortly after he came to his country."

He lifted a small picture from off the wall and showed it to him. There was a young man in it leaning against a barber pole wearing a stark white shirt holding a pair of scissors and a straight razor.

"Grand Poppa was just twenty there, he'd been cutting hair here for almost two years by then. This was just after the Civil War."

He took the picture and hung it back up where it had been.

"And that one there," he said pointing to another picture then went back to cutting his hair. "That's my Poppa on the right and my uncle on the left of their Poppa."

"No picture of you and your Poppa?" he asked knowing it might not be the best question to ask him.

"My Poppa and I," he began. "He didn't want me to cut hair. "You think you can find out who shot Pop Morre?"

It took him a second or two to realize that he had changed the subject. Out of the corner of his eye he spotted the girls out in front. Andrea was waving her arms over her head, and wiggling her body around. While Jane was doing her best to imitate what she was doing. He laughed at them then waved them in. Just as they stopped there was a loud crash of metal against metal then a second one just after that. Looking out he noticed that two cars had collided on the street and a third had crashed in to the back of one of them.

Looking quickly over their shoulders the two ran into the barbershop as the first two drivers began yelling at each other. They sat quickly in the seats in front of the window so they had their backs to the street. Dawson and the barber laughed as they slumped down to further conceal themselves. In the street traffic was quick to become snarled. Since it was a Saturday there were plenty of people around to attract to the accident. They were leaning out of windows and milling about the scene taking it all in. It wasn't long before more people were yelling and some began laying into their horns.

"Car Horn Concerto in E-Flat," Andrea laughed when the one horn became many.

"Steve," he began, "I want you to meet my assistants, Jane and Andrea."

"Which one is which?" he asked not taking his eye off of either of them.

"They're interchangeable," he said smiling at them just as Jane was about to tell him.

"Be careful," she started but it was too late he had already taken a bit of finger with his next cut.

He pulled his hand away and began cursing in a mix of Russian and Polish

"Every time, every time," he said wrapping his finger with a bandage. "Only today of all days I have two beautiful ladies in my shop and I have to cut myself and the hair."

"I hope you aren't charging me extra for that."

He went back to mumbling and cursing in Russian.

None of them could keep themselves from laughing. Jane was the first to get up and see if he was alright. He told her it happened from time to time, just one of the hazards of the job. Only his wife might not think it funny later when he told her.

The commotion outside had brought the cops and that meant Riley. The barber saw him and cursed again only this time he spit in Riley's direction when he finished. It was one of those spits that old women use when they see someone they don't like. However Steve had meant it, Dawson and company didn't fail to notice it.

With his finger bandaged he was about to begin again on Dawson when Riley walked through the door.

"Figures I'd find you close by," he said as entered. "Wherever there's a commotion you're not too far away."

"Certainly you can't blame me for what happened out there. I have been in here getting my haircut."

The girls each had their legs pulled up on their chair and were trying to hide themselves behind a newspaper.

"Maybe you have maybe you haven't how do I know."

"Because I just told you and because the barber here is my witness. And if you'll notice my hair cut is more than halfway finished. Then again I forget you don't think normal."

"I ought to bust you," he returned his hand twisting as he gripped his baton.

"I wouldn't think you would want to do that," he said nodding his head toward the rookie Benson. "You'd have way too much explaining to do."

"I can handle him," he said looking over his shoulder at the young cop standing outside."

"Maybe, but I don't think you'd be able to handle the thirty-two to the back of the head you'd get before you could swing that thing."

Andrea dropped one side of her paper and raised her dress high enough to show the pistol strapped to her thigh.

"She better have a permit for that," he said as he backed toward the door.

"I'm sure she has, and I bet it's signed by the Police Commissioner."

"You mean Uncle Charlie?" Andrea asked still hiding her face.

"How is Uncle Charlie?" Jane asked as she finally stopped shaking.

"Oh, he's grand," she replied making a muffled snort sound as she tried not to giggle.

Riley stormed out of the shop and began yelling at people on the street. Laughter filled the barber shop as they watched him leave. They didn't stop as he first pushed then shoved the crowd and drivers to get them to move along. A few minutes later the street was cleared and the traffic was moving once again.

"What can you tell me about the Pawnbroker, I mean Pop?" he asked as the barber began running some tonic through his hair.

"Pop is a good man," he began. "He has always been good to me and my Poppa before me. He's always looking out for the people. Sure some don't like him because of what he does. They like to say how he profits on people's problems. Only I know for a fact that he always does more than he should. Of course sometimes people sell him things that were stolen but he always tries not to buy it. If you find something that was taken from you he will give it back to you, and he will be out the money."

"Sounds a little generous to a fault for a pawn broker," Dawson returned as he checked out his new haircut. "Not bad, I'll have to come here again. Only how about next time we leave the blood out of it?"

"In that case," he said laughing, "next time you better leave your assistants at home."

"That isn't as easy you might think," Jane chimed in.

"Didn't Pop have any employees?" Andrea asked. "I see it's still all boarded up."

"No but he has a daughter that comes around from time to time. She lives in California or Florida I think. Mrs. Peters, she owns the dress shop on the other side, she says she has been trying to call her but the number she has is no good."

"Do the cops know about the daughter?"

"I don't think so, they never asked."

"You mean to tell me that they haven't talked to you yet about him or the shooting?" Andrea asked.

"No Miss, it's that Riley he's no good I tell you. Any police start asking questions about what goes on in this neighborhood Riley chases them off. He tells them that he's already asked all the questions. He either tells them that we won't talk or that we don't know nothing. I'm sorry; I mean to say he tells them we don't know anything."

"I was hoping I might be able to get a look around inside today," Dawson said paying him.

"Oh, that's no problem, wait here," he told them and ran out of the shop.

A minute later he was back with a key.

"It's to the back door, with Riley snooping around you're probably better off going in that way anyway."

"Who was it that boarded the place up?" Jane asked innocently.

"We all did," he told her. "That is the neighborhood did. Mrs. Peters had the same insurance people. They are only waiting for him to sign some papers so he can get a new window."

"They're going to be waiting a very long time," Dawson returned.

Steve looked puzzled at first. A second later he seemed to catch on as he lowered his head. Clasping his hands together he began to say a few words in Russian. Dawson slipped his hat off and they all bowed their heads. When he was finished he raised his head and crossed his body.

He asked them when it had happened, after telling him he thanked them. He told him that he would let everyone else in the neighborhood know. They all left the shop and he locked his door behind them before crossing the street.

"What are we going to do now?" Jane asked.

"We're going to look around of course," he said lighting a cigarette.

They followed him as he went to the alley beside the barber shop where he had taken cover. Examining the marks left by the bullets as they had hit the buildings he nodded every now and then.

"This isn't exciting," Jane complained. "This isn't exciting at all."

"Really," Andrea returned, "I find this fascinating."

"Well," Dawson began, "I'm sorry darling it isn't always fun and games. One has to put up with the boring to make the rest so exciting."

Once inside the pawnshop, the three of them started looking around. He wasn't sure what it was that he was looking for. He only knew that he was missing at least one piece of the puzzle and he hoped that one of them was there. Everything was the same as it had been two nights earlier the blood soaked shirts that he had used to help stem the flow of blood. The wrappings from the bandages that doctors had torn open, right down to the pen that had fallen from Pop's hand as he was shot.

"Do we know what we're looking for?" Andrea asked leaning against the counter.

"I wish I knew," he answered sitting down in a chair behind the counter.

The desk in front of him looked as if someone gone through it looking for something more than once. It was an old roll top desk probably made somewhere in the middle of the previous century. All of the drawers were open part way or all the way. His papers were strewn about it in a way that one might think the man had been very disorganized except, he wasn't. Dawson remember on every occasion that he had come into the shop his desk had been very neat. He had always seemed to know where everything was. If he told you he didn't have it, then he didn't have it. Whenever anyone had come in to pay off a loan all he needed to see was their ticket. Right away he knew the amount of the loan, the item and how long it had been in his shop. Every entry that he had ever seen in his ledger had been meticulous.

"His ledger," he said aloud as he began going through the mess on the desk.

The women looked at each other and then questioned his outburst.

He told them what he was looking for and why.

"So you think it may have been a robbery, and the rest just bad timing?" Andrea asked.

"Sort of," he answered. "Although I think there is more to it than just a simple robbery; a lot more."

After getting the street cleared for traffic again Riley walked to the corner of the street and waited for them. He watched as the women came out and then Dawson. He was about to have a talk with him when the barber followed them and went across the street. He wasn't sure what the barber was up to, but he had to find out what Dawson was up to.

"Why don't you go over to fortieth," Riley told his rookie partner. "Go see that old lady about the break in."

"Umm sure," Benson replied unsure as to why he would send him back over there. "I thought you said that you talked to her...."

"Just do what I tell ya," Riley returned angrily.

Shrugging his shoulders Benson took off in the direction of Fortieth Street.

As the trio went into the alley next to the building, Riley ran to the next street corner. He wasted no time in going around to the back of the corner building. Making his way quickly up the alley he hid in an alcove of the buildings back door. Grabbing at his revolver he watched as the three of them went in the back door of the pawnshop.

Joey Tuna leaned against his Cadillac as he watched two of his men walking from storefront to storefront. After the shootout the day before he wasn't about to let any of them get too far away without help close by. He even managed a smile as they would wave when they exited a store.

"Looks like we got us a new street here boys," he said aloud.

The three armed men in the back seat of the car chuckled as he spoke. Joey mentally counted the money as they went. He couldn't help but think about which street they should offer 'insurance' on next. He smiled as he reached into his shirt pocket for one of his cigars.

"It's good to be me," he said as he lit it, chuckling as he did so.

Exhaling, he saw Dawson stepping out of the barbershop down the street.

"Looks like my day just got a little bit better," he said exhaling as he saw Dawson stepping out of the Barbershop. "One of you boys, quick hand me my heater."

"What's up boss?" one asked.

He told them what he'd seen.

"You want we should take care of him," another said.

"No," he said taking the revolver from them. "He's all mine, he's a problem that goes way back."

He couldn't help but see Riley moving around the building as well. Not that he thought he was trying to not to be noticed. Maybe, he thought, I can get two problems out of my hair. He didn't hide the thirty-eight as he opened the cylinder. Reaching his hand back through the window he asked for bullets. He pulled out three spent shells and replaced them with fresh bullets.

"I'll be back," he told them as he took off toward the alley.

After finding his favorite early morning eating place Douglas Barnes took a short nap in the back while Mickey curled up against the driver's door and dozed as well. Three hours later right on time his alarm clock, the old woman that sold flowers on the street, knocked on the cars window waking the two men.

"I haven't seen you in a long time Mr. Barnes," the old woman said as he rolled down the back window.

"Almost two years," he smiled. "You still carry my usual?"

"Of course I do," she said handing him a small bouquet of white and red roses. "I always keep one just in case."

"You want one for Cook?" he asked.

Mickey made a sound, shook his head and as always when he mentioned the cook his face turned a shade of deep red.

Darla Bell had been selling flowers on the city's streets for as long as anyone could remember. He asked her how she was and about her children and grandchildren. She told him briefly that she had them all in the business now.

"Shirley asks if I see you every now and again," she said smiling. "You remember her don't you? She really enjoyed meeting you. Maybe you can take her out again. You know she needs to give me some grandchildren. There are more streets out there than I would like to sell on."

"Always thinking ahead you are," he laughed.

"What else I got to do but sell flowers and think ahead. I'm too old for anything else," she added throwing her head back in a good hearty laugh.

She shook her head and cursed as a shopkeeper tried to shoo her away.

He asked her if she had anything new to tell him

"I got nothing else for you now," she said as he handed her a double sawbuck.

He told her that it was alright and had her give him another bunch of flowers. Darla thanked him and made her way up the street, yelling back at the shopkeeper as she went. Tossing the second bunch of flowers into the front seat he told him that he wanted to go by the pawn shop on Thirty-Eighth Street. Twenty minutes later they were sitting in front of the pawnshop and Barnes was out on the street watching as Joey Tuna made his way toward the alley.

Tossing the desk one more time he looked again for the Ledger Pop wrote everything in. Jane was the first to find something that didn't belong where it was. Under a table a few feet away from where Pop laid the night of the shooting she found an empty box. Andrea found herself attracted as usual by the all the glittery things in the display case at the counter.

"Now that's pretty," she said pointing her finger at a bracelet.

"It's probably a fake," Jane laughed as she stood up the box in her hand. "Could this be something?"

"I don't think so Pinky," Andrea added using the name they used to call each other in school. "I know fake when I see them and this one's real."

She raised the box over her head and waited for an answer. He asked her where she found it, she told him. He told her that it could be and to hang on to it.

A minute later he found the book he was looking for under the desk.

"What a funny place to find that," he stood and walked to the counter flipping the pages of it as he went.

As he set book down on the counter two shots rang out in the store. Jane fell to the floor immediately. While Andrea dropped to one knee Dawson slumped over the counter. Standing back up she had her thirty-two in hand and was moving as fast as she could toward the back of the shop. She saw movement as the shooter made their way to the back door. Stopping she fired off three rounds.

"Dammit," she yelled as the door slammed shut behind whoever it was as they left the building.

Turning her attention to Dawson and Jane she called out for them both. Jane was the first to answer and told her that she was okay. Dawson lay with his upper body over the counter his legs folded as if he were sitting. Her hand touched the wound in his left shoulder as she reached to see if he was still breathing.

Before the women could check him out any further, more

shots rang out from the alley behind the shop. Leaving Jane to take care of him she went to the back door this time with both of her thirty twos. However, by the time she got to the alley there was no one there to see. When she returned Dawson was coming to.

As he touched the bloody crease in his temple he realized that he'd been a very lucky man. Although a second later he noticed that he wasn't that lucky as he felt the pain in his shoulder.

"Did you get'em?" Jane asked when she returned.

"Didn't even see who it was," she told her handing back the one convincer.

"I think we've over stayed our welcome on this street." He picked up his hat from the desk and put it on.

Wiping the blood from his forehead they told him they needed to get him to the hospital.

"Nah," he returned shoving a cigarette in his mouth. "I think it's time for a drink."

Jane laughed as she lit his cigarette before taking one for herself as well.

"Either of you ladies hungry," he said as they headed for the back door. "There's a great delicatessen a few blocks from here." He added pulling both automatics from their holsters.

"Don't be silly you're bleeding," Andrea told him as they made their way to the street.

He was more than a little disappointed when they hadn't run into whoever it was that had shot him. He had expected to at least bump into Riley before they reached the street again, but he was nowhere to be seen. The forty-five in his left hand clattered on the concrete sidewalk as it fell. Bending over he tried his best to pick it up, he had it in his hand three times before giving up. Andrea finally grabbed it and stuffed it back into its holster.

"Daddy's sorry he dropped you," he said patting the butt end of the gun with his right hand. "I didn't mean to drop you like that on that hard concrete sidewalk."

Waving the other automatic in the air they stepped to the curb, and he tried to whistle. As he tried to hail a cab Jane took the shop key to the barber and told him what had happened. Running out he looked at the crease in his forehead.

"Wait I'll get a doctor," he said.

"I would rather have a scotch or maybe some bourbon."

His eyes crossed as his knees gave out as he spoke. The girls caught him and with the barbers help they were able to get him into his shop. With him successfully seated in one of the barber chairs he picked up the phone and called for a doctor. As they waited they managed to get him undressed to his waist. Dawson came to again as they cleaned the wound on his forehead. A few minutes later the red headed doctor made her way into the shop.

"Ah the red head," he said lighting a cigarette. "Have I ever told you how much I love red heads?"

"Why is it that every time I see you it involves bullets and blood," she said looking at his shoulder, ignoring his words.

"I couldn't think of a way to be introduced yesterday." He smiled as he spoke trying to put on his best face. "So I had one of my assistants over there shoot me. They thought that the head shot would be enough but I told them that I didn't want you think I was some wet rag so I had the other one shoot me in the shoulder. Just so I could have another opportunity to meet you."

"I suppose if I had been the coroner you would have had them kill you."

"I might have thought about it, but in the end I am sure that it would have only been a one sided introduction," he continued extending his right hand. "My name is…"

"Dawson yes I know," she said stopping him. "Everyone in the neighborhood talks about you."

"Aw now you're just flattering me."

"You really need to be in the hospital for this," she told him as she looked at his shoulder.

"Nonsense just get me some good rye whiskey and you can fix it right here." Reaching over his shoulder he felt the hole in it.

"If you're too squeamish I probably could dig it out for you. I might need two bottles for that though."

"Any excuse for you to get tight right dear," Jane added heavily accentuating dear as if she were marking her territory.

"Now that is so unlike you Jane," he laughed reaching to snub out his cigarette. "Retract your claws, I am sure the good Doc is only concerned with my head and shoulder and not everything else that goes with it. Reach in my jacket then go get some good hooch, we're going to need a sterilizer."

"I think I have enough for my instruments."

"I'm not worried about that," he added as she touched his shoulder again. "I'm worried that there isn't enough for me. Maybe you better make it bourbon, yeah bourbon for shoulder and head wounds."

Andrea grabbed his billfold out of his jacket giving it to Jane as she pushed her toward the door. With the news that Pop had died spreading through the neighborhood and now that Dawson had been shot there was a small but growing crowd outside of the barber shop.

Rookie beat cop Officer Carl Benson pushed his way through the crowd and looked through the shop window. Jane pushed her way past him and hailed a cab. There was a lot of talk about the death of Pop and the shooting rippling through the crowd. Along with speculation as to who had done both. Stepping inside Benson asked what had happened.

"You see it's like this," Dawson said smiling through the probing that the doctor was giving him. "I saw this beautiful red head here yesterday and I had no way to meet her."

"I know what you and everyone in the neighborhood thinks of Riley," he returned trying not to be upset by him not giving him a straight answer. "I know that no one thinks much of me because I have been partnered with him, but I'm really..."

"You just couldn't wait until I got here could you," Abrams yelled as he stepped into barber shop. "It's alright Officer I'll take it from here."

Benson was about to protest but thought better of it. Instead he turned and sulked as he went back out into the street. He did his best to shoo away crowd that were trying to get a look inside at what was happening.

"You should go a little easier on the boy," he told him feeling a little guilty himself. "It's not his fault that he has Riley for a partner."

Abrams told him that he would keep it mind and see about making it up to him later.

"Now you want to tell me how it is that you're sitting here with Doc Dennison probing your shoulder?"

He told him everything, except what he had figured out from looking around in the shop.

"What do you make of it?" the detective asked him.

"Unless I miss my guess I think that whoever it was that shot our Mr. Morre didn't much like me snooping around."

"Well you aren't exactly on top of everyone's Christmas list."

"I don't know what you're talking about. Everyone …" he returned as she pulled the bullet from his shoulder. "It's about time."

His eyes rolled back in his head and he fell back against the barber chair.

"I figured that would shut him up," she said as she held the bloody bullet up in the jaw of her forceps.

Placing the bullet onto the offered towel by the barber she went back to treating the wound. Moving quickly she cleaned and sewed his wounds shut while he was still passed out from the pain. With Andreas help it didn't take very long.

"It's a lot easier when they aren't running off at the mouth," she laughed when she was finished.

"One thing about him," Andrea added, "he's got something to say for just about anything."

"And just about enough answers for it to," Abrams added laughing.

"Which one of you slipped me the Mickey," he said groggily as he came to again a minute later. "How about a snipe?"

Abrams found his cigarettes and tossed him the pack.

"My savior has arrived," he said lighting a cigarette as Jane entered the shop carrying a bottle of bourbon.

"I have to say though you are a pretty tough character," the Doctor said. "I don't know anyone that didn't yell out at least once while I was digging into them for a bullet."

"He's really a softy," Andrea said. "I think he was just trying to impress you."

"Did it work?" he asked her.

"See what I mean Doc," Abrams added.

She packed her medical bag and tried not to smile.

"Well you impressed me darling," Andrea told him as she handed him a drink.

Leaning in she kissed him on the cheek.

"Hey, now let's not get too mushy over good bourbon."

They all laughed as Jane helped him get dressed. He looked at himself in the mirror and had to chuckle at the site of the bandage over his left eye and his left arm in a sling.

"Walking wounded," he said taking another drink. "Who could ask for anything more?"

"I think the ladies and I would have preferred it if you weren't one of the walking wounded," Abrams added.

Smiling he asked Jane to pay Doc Dennison.

"I'll send you my bill," she said holding up her hand to Jane.

Reaching in the billfold he pulled out a half century and handed to the barber. He told him it was for the use of the hall. The barber refused it at first. Then all he could hear was what his wife was going to say when he told her about it that night. Eventually he took the note and thanked him for it, although he was sure that there was a chance he would make more than that in the next few days as the neighborhood came by to hear about everything that happened. His barbershop would be famous for a while and that made him smile.

"I'm feeling a little peckish," he said. "I think it's time for something to eat."

"Would you like to join us Sarah?" Andrea asked of the doctor.

Declining she claimed to have other patients to see in the neighborhood. On the way out Abrams told them that he would drive.

"Haven't the doors fallen off that tin can yet?" Dawson asked. "I nearly fell through the floor last time I took a ride with you."

"You've got nothing to worry about this time," Abrams laughed as he remembered the incident. "Thanks to your idea yesterday that is."

He asked him what he meant and Abrams told him.

"We found another one of Joey's men standing next to a brand new Lincoln around the corner. It belongs to the department, for now at least."

He saw Benson standing on the corner talking to one of the local teenagers. Calling him over, he apologized to the beat cop for having been short with him. Then he asked him if he knew where Riley had gotten to. He told the detective that he had no idea where he was.

"Well, I think you've been a beat cop long enough," he told the Rookie. "I'm going to need a driver, are you up to it?"

The Rookie wasn't sure what to do, but Abrams assured him he would call his station and make it right.

"To the Delicatessen Chester," Dawson called from the back seat when the three of them were settled in. "And don't spare the horses my good man."

Leaning back he took a long drink from his bottle.

"You better take it easy on that stuff," Jane told him taking the bottle from him. "You've lost a lot of blood. Replacing it with bourbon isn't the best idea. After you get something to eat we'll take you home where you can get some rest."

"Don't they tell you to drink a lot after you give blood?"

"Maybe," Andrea replied, "but I am pretty sure they don't mean bourbon."

"I thought you were the fun one," he said giving her a shove.

Benson pulled the car to the curb a few doors past the Delicatessen.

"I hope you haven't eaten lunch yet," Abrams said to Benson.

"That's good," Dawson said when he told them no. "It's your turn to buy Chester."

"My turn," Abrams protested, "How is it my turn? Didn't I buy yesterday?"

"You were supposed to," Dawson laughed, "but with your little shoot out and all you forgot."

"Wait a minute," Abrams said as they were about to enter the Deli. "Abraham told us we didn't have to pay yesterday so that means ..."

"That means it's still your turn," Jane added taking the rookie cops arm.

"I'm not so sure about that," Abrams said scratching his head.

"Well Abrams," he added laughing "When you figure it out you let me know."

"He's got you dead to rights on this one Chester," Andrea laughed.

"My wife's gonna kill me," he returned shaking his head and mentally counting his roll.

Daniel came out from behind the counter to welcome them. Smiling he asked about the new wounds Dawson was sporting.

"I slipped in the tub this morning," he told him. "The girls wanted me to show them my swan dive."

Jane however insisted on telling him what had really happened.

"Excuse me," Dawson said stepping around them. "I've been through this movie already, it's a drama, and I like comedies."

Abrams went to the phone as she continued to tell the young man from her point of view what had happened. When he was connected to the precinct he asked for Benson's Captain. While he waited Andrea came over offered him a cigarette and asked him for his order. He told her what he wanted while taking the offered cigarette. Lighting it he waited for the Captain to come on the line.

While they waited for their lunch and for Abrams to return, Dawson asked the rookie cop if he had any thoughts on what had happened two nights earlier. He seemed to think a moment before answering but in the end Benson said that he didn't.

"I can see the gears turning," he told him. "There's something rattling around in the part of your head that Riley didn't screw up. You can talk around them. They're unofficially my official assistants."

Benson smiled and looked around them towards the phone booth where Abrams was sitting.

"You can speak your mind with him too, only I would wait for him to ask you first. That is unless I ask you before he does."

Looking around he squirmed in his chair for a minute as he fought his conscience.

"I only met him once, but I would never be able to trust him." Andrea said finally, trying to help him make up his mind. "He seems like the kind of flatfoot that has his thumb print on every apple on his beat."

Benson couldn't keep from laughing. Leaning back he nearly fell into the girl that was bringing their sandwiches. As she set them down she looked over at Daniel as if looking for his approval. He smiled and nodded then jerked his head toward the counter. After she left them Benson leaned in losing his smile.

"I couldn't be sure but from the way he acts he has more than his thumb print on apples." Benson relaxed a bit and took a sip of his coffee. "My pop was a cop, and a good one, he's retired now. I tell him about some of the things I see Riley doing. He says he's up to something. Pop's pretty sure that he's on the take, possibly even in a few hip pockets. I've got no proof understand but he's definitely up to something."

"So, do you think he had anything to do with the shooting of the Pawnbroker?" Dawson asked pouring a long jigger of bourbon in his coffee. "Doesn't taste as good as Irish but it'll do."

The coffee helped him keep awake with his body wanting to shut down, while the bourbon was helping the pain that was rising in him.

"I'm sure I don't know as much about it as you do," he began again.

"Hey kid," Abrams called form the phone booth. "You're Captain wants to talk to you for a minute."

He excused himself and went over the phone. As he handed him the phone Abrams told him that he was all set. The conversation between them was short with Benson replying with either a 'yes sir' or 'no sir', when the Captain was finished he thanked him. Looking at Abrams who had stood by the booth as they spoke he gave one more 'yes sir' before handing the phone back to him. Abrams gave him a pat on his shoulder as the officer stood up and went back to the table. Sitting down he told them that Abrams was good at his word and he was now on assignment to detective squad as whatever Abrams needed him to do. They congratulated the young officer and shook his hand.

"I guess that means that you can officially be filled in on anything that you don't know," Andrea said when they were done with the accolades.

"However dear," Dawson interrupted "I think we should wait and let that be at the discretion of Abrams."

Abrams came back in time to catch the end of the sentence.

"What am I using or not using my discretion on," he said sitting down.

"Your new protégé was about to tell us his thoughts on the Morre shooting and the subsequent snuff out of same."

Benson lowered his head unsure if he should continue or not, but Abrams didn't let him off the hook.

"Go ahead kid," he told him. "I'd kinda like to hear what you have to say about it myself."

"Well," he began with mouth full of his roast beef sandwich. "It don't look right to me."

He finished chewing and swallowed before elaborating.

"Sorry," he began again, "I'm not used to eating and talking around anyone but my Pop and he talks the same way so we understand each other."

"Never mind" Jane told him a little sympathetically. "I like a man that feels comfortable enough around me to be impolite."

"She must really like you a lot kid," Dawson added smiling, pouring more bourbon in his coffee. "She's never told me that and I'm impolite around her all the time."

She gave him a look that told him she would have a few words to share with him later.

"Anyway," Benson began catching the look and wanting to keep them from having the words right there. "Like I said before I am sure I don't know as much as you do about it, but I don't think those trigger men for Joey Tuna shot him. I think he was shot before the car came around the corner or at the same time."

"What makes you say that?" Abrams asked him.

"The way the bullets hit the front of the shops," he said sounding sure of himself. "They ricocheted up and away from the street. Not straight in like you'd need to hit someone inside. Besides if it was all about a protection scheme then they wouldn't want to kill him. They only started collecting today so it wasn't as if he owed them and wouldn't pay up."

"Okay," Abrams interrupted, "but what if this Morre was the hold up in the link. You know keeping the other shop owners from giving in. Wouldn't they want to kill him then? What if he had threatened to come to us and tell us what they were doing?"

"To be honest," he said. "I think he did come to us. Well to Riley anyway."

"So you think Riley is on the take?" the detective asked his interrogation voice slipping out as he talked. "Do you think he told Riley what was going on and Riley just ignored it?"

"Maybe," he nodded. "I got no proof of it mind you. It's just what me and my Pop figure, but I trust his intuition. He was twenty-five years on the job."

Abrams tilted his head and looked hard at the rookie.

"Now Chester there's no use in grilling the boy," Dawson said lighting a cigarette.

Having finished his sandwich the girl that had served them

immediately came and picked up the empty plates. Not saying a word she filled his coffee and made a quick check of the rest them.

"I love the service here," he added as she disappeared again behind the counter.

"It is rather good isn't it," Andrea said watching the girl retreat from the table.

"And quite the little cutie too," Jane added with the others nodding their agreement.

"You and your Pop aren't the first to think that maybe Riley is in a hip pocket or two," Abrams said finally getting back to the problem at hand. "It all comes down to proof doesn't it, but like you point out there isn't anyone that can say they have any. You think there's a chance he could have been the one to shoot Morre?"

"Again I couldn't say for sure, but he did say that he took three shots at the car as it went past the pawnshop that night. I was too far away to be sure if he hit anything or not with the rain and all."

"You weren't with him when it happened," Abrams asked.

"No he sent me down Thirty-Sixth Street; told me he was going to do a check on some kid that was on probation. I didn't think nothing of it, he does it all time so I never checked the time or thought anything different than normal."

"Then how do you know for sure that he fired at the car?"

"I guess I don't," he returned. "But he said that he did and he was replacing three bullets in his revolver when I caught up with him."

Dawson and Abrams looked at one another then back at the rookie cop. Neither said anything, but they both knew what the other was thinking.

"Now for the big question," Dawson said. "Do you think there's a chance that he could have put the slug in me today?"

"He was around alright, then again so weren't a lot people." He shrugged his shoulders and took another bite of his sandwich.

After swallowing the bite he told them that he'd seen Joey hanging out nearby. Almost as an afterthought he told them about another guy he'd never seen before.

"He was getting into the back seat of a brand new Lincoln," he added. "There was another man sitting in the driver's seat wearing a chauffeur's hat."

He stuffed the last bite of his sandwich in his mouth and followed it with a sip of coffee.

"Hell," he said again through a mouth full of roast beef. "For all I know it could have been the girl I seen coming out of the end of the alley when I saw you three coming around by the barber shop."

"I think you're going to do just fine kid," Dawson said snubbing out his cigarette.

When he was done the girl came over to the table picked up the ashtray replacing it with a clean one.

"She's attentive, you gotta give her that much," he smiled at the girl as she backed away.

"My kid sister, well I found her on my doorstep a while back, and I sort of adopted her as my kid sister anyway." Daniel said rubbing the top of her head for a second as he came to the table. "Mr. Dershowitz I mean Abraham wanted me to thank you two again for yesterday. The only thing is that little bit really isn't going to stop them from coming in here or anywhere else in the city to collect protection money. If it were me I wouldn't be thanking you, but I'm not him. All you two did was make it harder on him the next time they come. The only way you're going to stop them is to put them all in prison."

"I'm with you there," Abrams spoke up. "That means that when we get these mugs in a lineup the business owners need to step up and point their fingers at who's doing the collecting. We can figure out from there who they work for and hopefully pin something on them. Taking out their muscle one or two at a time might be slow, but eventually they'll start to see it'll cost them more to stay in the racket than it's worth."

"You mean hopefully," Dawson added. "Don't let yourself

forget the odd kiss off some the business owners get when they do step up. No my friend you have to cut the snake off at the head in order for that to do any good. The only problem there is that once you cut off one head another snake always comes along to take its place."

He pulled his bottle out and was about to pour some more into his coffee cup when Jane, Andrea and Abrams gave him one of those looks that told him that perhaps he had better not Shrugging off the look he put the cap back on the bottle and put it back in his pocket..

"Listen Daniel," he started again. "You're young, from what I can gather you have some smarts too. Only I don't really think you see the whole picture. You can't just expect that everyone is on the same page with this. No one wants to pay these hoods, but they do and they take abuse knowing what will happen if they don't or if they pick them out of a line up. They all have their own reasons for paying up. Abraham pays them so that they don't hurt the kids that work here. Mrs. Holiday that has the hat shop on the corner pays them so they don't break her windows or stop her from getting her supplies. The hardware store pays them so that the trucks can bring in their lumber and nails without problems. You see what I'm getting at? They all have their own reasons for paying them. Me I got no reason to pay them so I don't and wouldn't anyway, but that's me. You, well you didn't have a reason to pay them until yesterday when you stepped up for Abraham. Now you'll pay them so they won't hurt any of the kids. It's your job to see they stay safe now. You know they'll be back, even Abraham knows they'll be back. That doesn't mean that he isn't thankful that we were here and stopped those two from collecting yesterday. We'd have followed them outside if we could have. That is if it weren't for them slapping him around. You see, you can push a man around for a long time before he'll tell you when he's had enough, but you slap him around once and he'll spend the rest of his life finding a way to get even. And for Abraham that would have ended with him dead on the floor just like Bradley King was yesterday. You see he didn't thank us for stopping them from collecting exactly. He thanked us for stepping up and getting even for him."

Daniel lowered his head as he turned and walked away from the table. Abrams had been surprised at what the young man had said, but to hear his friend admonished him made him feel a little uneasy. It was as if he had witnessed a parent telling his child what the facts were after they had lied to them. It may all have been true but something told him that Daniel wasn't looking at it that way.

"I think I may have just over stayed our welcome." He stood up slowly and unsteady as he spoke.

The pain in his shoulder and head where still letting him know that they weren't going anywhere soon, but the booze had taken the edge off it; for now anyway. His head spun a little more than he had expected, taking a few side steps he regained his balance.

Abrams watched and fought back a chuckle as he asked the young girl how much he owed for lunch.

"Already taken care of old man," Dawson said holding his head with his good hand. "Now if I can keep my head still long enough I think I can make it outside."

He took a step backwards and the young girl that had waited on them was immediately at his side. Her arm wrapped around his waist as she lifted his good arm over her shoulder. Not letting go of him she helped him to the door.

"Very attentive," he said as Jane took over for her when they reached the door.

Turning around he called her back. Thanking her he gave her a checker and kissed her cheek for her help. The twelve year old blushed and smiled but still said nothing.

He told her to keep an eye on her big brother before turning and heading out the door.

"Thanks again," Daniel called from the counter.

Dawson stuck his head back in the door and smiled. Nodding his head once he gave him a wink as if to say he was going to do just fine

"I don't suppose you're up to a drive?" Abrams asked him as they were stepping into his car.

"Where too?" he asked looking over his shoulder.

"I got a lead on where Joey's typists are hiding out until things cool down."

"Not today mister," Andrea said pushing him the rest of the way in the car. "They'll still be there tomorrow."

"Actually by tomorrow we might have them downtown if we can swing it."

"I don't think that will do you much good in finding out who it was that shot Mack," he said settling in the back seat. "Then again you can charge them for shooting up the street. I don't think my going out there will do much good. If you still have them tomorrow I might have a question or two for them but I am sure you will have already asked them."

He told him that he would let him know what he found out from them. Dawson was asleep before they reached his apartment building. It took the help of the doorman to get him out of the car. With Benson and Abrams help the girls managed to get him the rest of the way to his apartment. After they left the girls undressed him and rolled him into his bed. Pouring a drink they sat listening to the radio and talking until the sun finally set.

Safely back in her room Carolyn, now Abbey counted herself lucky that she hadn't been caught by either Joey or Riley. It had been close though, too close really.

"You get everything you needed?" Karen asked opening her door.

She told her that she had and asked when she thought she'd be able to get her 'friends' to go by and pick up the rest of her things.

"You just say the word," she told her. "They can pick them up tonight if you want."

She told her that it would be fine and that she had made a list of things that were hers that she wanted to keep. The rest she said either belonged to the apartment or she no longer wanted.

"How much back rent you owe them?" she asked as she was about to leave.

She said that she wasn't behind, and it was true, in fact she was a couple of weeks ahead.

"Whenever you're ready I can get one of the girls to teach you how to use the switch board so you can start work. It might not be glamorous but it is legit. Well mostly legit anyway."

"Why not now," she returned, hoping to keep her mind occupied.

They joked and laughed as they made their way to the room under the street. It wouldn't take her long to learn that the problem with working for a 'pick-up service', that's what Karen had called it, is that it gives you too much time to think. That night Abbey couldn't help but think about her life and how it was that she ended up there hiding from three men. Two that wanted nothing more than to use her and the third she was sure would never want anything to do with her again. He was bound to find out eventually, although she had thought that she would be the one to tell him when the time was right. Like maybe when they were older and watching their grandchildren running around on the lawn.

Almost everyone she knew wanted out of something, out of the slums, out of the city, out of the life that they had been born into. She wasn't any different, only she had no idea of the best way to go about it. It was easy to make the promise that she would never wind up married and living in some rundown apartment with bad or no plumbing at all. The hard part would be in making it happen.

With her big brown eyes and brunette hair that she liked to wear to the middle of her back, she was always told that she was 'as cute as a bug's ear'. Her eyes were always bright and full of innocence and a passion for life. When she was ten she talked her way into working in a delicatessen several blocks from her home. It was there that she that changed her name for the first time. The owner and his wife were good to her. They fed her and even made her go to school. Still she knew that working there was not going to get her the better life she wanted.

It wouldn't be too long before that changed too. On her way home from the deli one night she met a woman, Cecelia Robbins, and she promised that she could help her get that better life that she wanted. As long as she stuck with her she would never go hungry and never be without a place to live. She turned her first trick a day later when she was just fourteen. However, over the six years that she was a 'working girl' two things never happened. During that time she was never arrested and she never did any of the drugs that the other girls were into. Admittedly however she did like to drink and she would get a little tight from time to time. Sometimes more often than she wanted, but in a way that was part of the life.

It wasn't always easy but she saved her money as best she could. Whenever she would get a 'gift' she would hide it away. If it was jewelry and it usually was, she would wear it once or twice around the man that had given it to her. After that it was off to a safe place away from her life so that when she was ready she would be able to sell it. They didn't always give her the best stuff but she still hid it away for her better life. There were a couple of times that she had to use some of it, once to bail out Cecelia and the other girls, although she had paid her back.

She met Douglas Barnes in a speakeasy across town on her twentieth birthday. Some of the girls had taken her there to celebrate. They'd all watched him as he came through the door. Even joked at how out of place he looked. While the others continued to make fun of him she couldn't take her eyes off him. He was sitting at a table near the edge of the dance floor with a girl and another couple. Announcing that she was going to dance she pulled one of her friends with her. Managing to bump into him a few times she would make her apology but he didn't once look at her. Not satisfied with that, on the third number after he still hadn't looked up, she politely, but not so innocently fell into his lap.

"Well hello there," he'd said when he found her arms around his neck.

"Hello yourself," she smiled back before getting up and returning to the dance floor.

One thing was sure that got his attention. She could feel his eyes watching her as she laughed with her friends and finished the dance. A few minutes later when the woman with him got up from their table, he came over to them and introduced himself.

"I always like to know the names of the girls that sit in my lap," he said sitting down next to her. "My name is Barnes, Douglas Barnes. However, you can call me anything you want just as long as you don't call me Doug."

She told him her name was Carolyn Walsh, which it wasn't. It also wasn't the name she had been using at the time. She didn't care; she only knew that from that second on she didn't want to live without him in her life. The next day she told Cecelia that she quit. Three days later she left the house where she worked after burning everything that had any name on it that she had used in her past.

The phone rang and brought her out of her thoughts.

"Karen's pick-up service, when you're not home we pick up." she said into the phone.

She gave the caller their messages and hung up. Not wanting to go back to those thoughts she got up and poured herself a drink and lit a cigarette. She had all but quit smoking when she'd changed lives. The only time she would smoke now was if she was around a bunch of people that smoked or if she had a drink. She was on her way to getting tight when the next girl came in to relieve her. She recognized the girl, but if the other girl knew her she didn't let on.

After exchanging polite greetings she told the girl what she needed to know about any calls she needed to make.

"Oh, Abbey," the girl said as she was about to leave. "Karen wanted me to tell you that she is having a party upstairs if you wanted to go up."

"I doubt it," she said thanking the girl.

"I would be up there still," she said smiling. "Those boys sure know how to show a girl a good time."

"If I know Karen," Abbey returned, "they can afford to."

"You ain't just a kiddin' honey," she added fanning herself with a number of bills. "Zowee, you ought to go and get you some too."

The offer was tempting and she did think about as she made her way back to her new apartment. How long would she be able to survive off what she would make answering phones? With Pop dead she had no idea who she could trust to sell more of her jewelry. After last night she was sure that Douglas would want nothing more to do with her. His mother had pegged her right from the start. She was nothing but a floozy, to use the polite term his mother had used. She'd even called her a gold digger, even though she had a lot of money in jewelry in a way she guessed she was right about that too.

It was close to three in the morning and the party on the top floor was in full swing. Down in the small room in the basement Abbey finally cried herself to sleep.

Douglas Barnes made it home about mid-afternoon. When he asked he was told that Carolyn had gone riding early that morning and hadn't returned. After having his horse saddled he went out looking for her. It didn't take him long to find her horse eating grass in the meadow where she'd left him. Shortly after that he found where she had changed her clothes. He knew then that she had run off.

Some hours later Mickey entered the library where Douglas had been since returning to the house.

"What do you want me to do with this?" he asked holding the satchel of cash from that morning.

He asked him if he'd checked it yet. He told him that he hadn't. Waving him over to the desk he said that they might as well do it now. Going through the bills one at a time they checked to make sure they were real. It wouldn't have been the first time Joey had paid for drugs with counterfeit bills. They added it up and wrote the amount on a piece of paper. While he put the money in a square bundle Mickey went to the kitchen for some string and butcher paper. Once the money was wrapped and tied he stuck the paper with the amount on it under the string.

"Where do you think we should donate this one too?" he asked his chauffeur.

"I think it might be time we donated it to ourselves," he laughed.

"I'm not so sure that would be right," he told him.

"Maybe your right," Mickey said looking rejected.

"Then again I can't see any harm in a little off the top." He laughed as he tossed the big man two stacks of the notes. "Here's a little for your retirement."

Mickey smiled as he caught them. He'd never said anything about the money that they had gotten before and didn't expect anything from it.

"You sure about this boss?" he asked. "You know I was only kidding about donating it to us."

"I know," he said, "Now why don't you go thank Cook for that box."

After turning red and agreeing with him Mickey left him alone in his library. Writing a name and address on the bundle of cash he locked it up in a drawer of his desk. Pouring himself a drink, he turned on the radio and sat down on the long leather couch. Lighting a cigar he picked up the book he'd been reading a few days earlier. He made no pretense of reading it as he sipped his drink and puffed on his cigar. All he could do was think about her and where she had gone. Reminding himself to make a call in the morning he lay his head back and finally fell asleep.

The following morning Dawson woke in his bed with a half-naked body on either side of him, each with their head on his chest and an arm draped over him.

"I might be able to think of better ways to wake up, but not many," he whispered aloud. "And they said I was wasting my money when I bought such a big bed."

The thrum of his head reminded him of the crease he'd gotten the day before. Reaching out trying not to disturb either woman he grabbed the pack of cigarettes and ashtray from the night stand. Putting the ashtray on his chest he lit a cigarette and tried to put a few things together. It had started out as just a normal case of curiosity for him. He had crossed paths with Tuna a few times before but something told him that it wasn't one of his men that shot the pawnbroker, at least not directly. Although Tuna or one his boys may have put the slug in his shoulder. After all he and Abrams had to have hurt him a little when they took out Calluchi and King at the delicatessen. It didn't take him long to decide that the only way he was going to be happy now was to step into it with both feet. Besides, the two bullets fired at him had made it personal. Still it could wait, for now he was happy right where he was.

Andrea woke first about an hour later. She was apologetic for having slept on him at least until she noticed that Jane was in the same position.

"I must have been comfortable enough," he whispered.

She smiled at him while running her fingers through her hair.

"Well," she said sliding higher in the bed. "You were a very tempting site that much I can tell you for sure."

She kissed his cheek and took the cigarette from his fingers. After taking a long drag from it she asked him how he felt.

Rubbing his shoulder he told her that all things considered he felt great.

"Then again maybe it's just waking up between two gorgeous half naked women," He smiled and took the cigarette back from her.

She chuckled and ran her fingers through her hair again. Reaching out she stroked Jane's hair waking her gently.

"Come on sleepy head let's go get our man some breakfast."

"Since when did he become our man," she said sleepily.

"Last I knew I wasn't even sure if he was my man."

"Never mind that now," she added as they headed for the door. "How about we just get breakfast?"

Andrea smacked her bottom, Jane returned the favor and the two shrieked with laughter as they went out of the room.

Sitting on the edge of the bed he watched as they went out. Shaking his head he asked himself how he'd gotten into this mess in the first place. He decided the safest place for him was the shower. Pulling the bandage off his forehead and shoulder he checked both wounds in the mirror.

"Not bad, not bad at all," he whispered as he stepped into the shower. "I'll have to remember her for the next time I need a doctor."

After breakfast he sat listening to the girls chatter on about what they were going to do and what had happened the day before. Sipping his coffee and smoking a cigarette he planned his day. He needed to find the girl, he was sure that she was the pin that held it all together.

Filling two flasks and sticking them in his spare overcoat he double checked his automatics. His shoulder stiffened and the pain reminded him that it hadn't gone anywhere. As he was about to put his holsters over his shoulder he noticed the chunk the bullet had torn out of the left side. It wasn't enough to affect it but it was enough that it would bother the hole in his shoulder. After pointing it out Andrea added another bandage to his shoulder while Jane rapped a rag around the strap of the holster.

"We'll have to call you hunchback Dawson from now on," she laughed as she admired her handy work.

When he was ready he called down to the garage.

"Bert," he said when they answered. "Can you dig out my car and have it ready in ten minutes?"

He listened as they told him that it had two flat tires and that the battery was dead.

"We meant to fix it, but since you're supposed to be out of town," Bert said on the other end. "Well you know how it is things just got away from us. We'll have it ready this afternoon though."

He wasn't happy about it and let him know it in a way that left no doubt. Giving them two hours to have it in the condition they were supposed to have been keeping it in he slammed the phone down. Andrea sat at the table as he talked on the phone checking and reloading her thirty-two's.

"What do you think you're doing?" he asked her when he noticed her.

"What does it look like?"

"You think you're coming with me?"

"Think, no," she returned. "I am coming with you."

He protested but she reminded him that he had been wounded just the day before.

"You need someone to keep an eye on you." She told him. "Jane can stay here, go shopping, or go home, but the twins and I'll be going out that door with you."

Realizing that she was serious and there was nothing he could do short of shooting her he gave in.

"Alright," he said. "But you'll do everything I say when I say and with no questions."

"Yes sir," she smiled giving him a salute.

Jane tried to protest throughout it all, but realized that it wasn't going to do her any good. Giving in to it she decided that she would run home for a few things and then come back.

"I might even break down and make you dinner," she said putting on a 'brave' smile.

He leaned in and kissed her forehead.

"Now you behave," he told her.

She growled at him as he gave her head a pat.

"Careful I bite," she laughed. "Aren't you at least going to call Abrams?"

"No," he said, "I don't think he's going to like seeing what may happen today."

"I don't think I like the sound of that," she said.

"Oh goodie," Andrea added rubbing her hands together,

"more excitement!"

"What did I get myself into," he said looking up at the ceiling.

The girls laughed as they all left the apartment.

"Anything interesting today?" he asked the doorman as they stepped out and onto the sidewalk.

"You on the job?" he asked. "I thought you was retired?"

He nodded at the doorman.

"I ain't seen nothing too interesting," he returned. "Then I weren't looking for nothing either. I will from now on though."

He thanked him as he blew his whistle for a cab. Putting Jane in the first one he waited until it pulled away before whistling for the next one.

"How're you doing today Dawson?" the driver said as they settled in the back.

He looked at the cabbie tilted his head and squinted his eyes a little before he recognized him.

"Johnny, Johnny Cohen," he said half surprised to see him. "Been a long time, how are you doing, how's the wife and kids?"

"Yeah it's been a long time you and your brother sent me up for an eight year stretch," he said. "My misses is okay, some days I think she wishes I was still up river. Most of the kids are all grown up now. I'm gonna be a grandfather soon."

"It was nothing personal," Dawson returned.

"Aw that's alright Dawson I don't blame you, I got a dime from the judge. I did eight and they let me out with rest on parole. Best thing that ever happened to me really. Straightened my nose out really nice."

"I'm glad to hear that," he said looking over at Andrea.

"What do you know about a girl named Sally Masters?" he asked him.

Johnny thought for a bit and scratched his head. Taking off his cap he tapped it on the steering wheel. After a few seconds he admitted that he hadn't heard of her.

"At least I don't think so," he said. "Where am I taking you two lovely people?"

"I hope you don't have anything else planned today," he

said. "I think we'd better keep you for a while."

"Nah, I got nothing to do but try to make a living."

"Good," he smiled trying to get comfortable. "You know where Little Johnnies Hideaway Club is."

"Sure," he said. "It's a long way out you planning on keeping me when you get out there?"

"No sense changing horses, at least not until the race is done."

"Then you mind if I stop and call the misses. No tellin when we'll be getting back."

"As a matter of fact I do mind Johnny," he told him.

"Okay, Dawson, I understand."

"If it starts getting late when we're out there you can call her from there. Hell I'll even pay for the call."

"How do you know those three are still out there?" she asked him.

"Abrams would have called last night if he had them locked up."

"You trust this guy?" Andrea whispered after agreeing.

"Not as far as I can throw him," he returned shaking his head. "Tell me something, where'd you get all your moxie from?"

"My father is an old Army mule," she laughed. "I was about three months old when he dragged me and momma with him. First stop was the Philippines. Taught me how to clean a gun when I was three, shoot when I was five. Slapped two Derringers to my legs when I was six, momma thought he was crazy. They were forever arguing about him teaching me to shoot and making me carry them. That is until I was seven and we were in Arizona, I came home from school and found two men had broken into the house. They had momma all tied up, I told them that they needed to untie her and leave or I was going to shoot them. They laughed; I guess they thought I was funny. Of course they didn't believe that such a cute little girl would know what a gun was let alone be able to shoot one. They didn't think it was so funny after I made one of them a soprano and the other one walk with a permanent limp for the rest of his life. After that day momma never said another word to daddy about the guns. As I grew up the guns got bigger and more powerful. Gave the twins to me for my high school graduation, they're my favorites."

"Remind me not get you mad at me." He lit a cigarette and looked at her again and offered her one.

"What got you into the detective business?" she asked taking the offered smoke.

"Can't say as if I can put a finger on it really," he said lighting her cigarette.

Pulling out one of the flasks and taking a sip he thought about it for a second or two before telling her more.

"The old man's a Marine," he began. "Everything with him is by the book. He's hard, but then again it's all he knows, Grand Pop was a Marine too, and so wasn't his father before him. So you get a good idea where that goes. The Colonel likes to say that it was our family what invented the Marines, Navy as well. Family gatherings can be quite a site. That is until one side gets drunk and picks a fight with the other side. Then it's all hands on deck. Anyway Grand Pop retired out as a Colonel, he was an investigator for about fifteen of the forty some odd years he was in. If there was an accident or killing or theft he was called in to solve it. The old man always said that wasn't really being a Marine. Maybe that's why I got interested what the Colonel did, because it wasn't being a Marine. I got nothing bad to say about being a Marine I just didn't think it was for me. Needless to say he wasn't very happy when I didn't follow along with the family tradition. The Colonel taught me everything he knew about investigating and from there it just seemed to happen. I was fifteen when an old friend of his came by to get his help with a case. Only his legs weren't very good then. So he ended up getting me to leg it out for him. Told him everything I saw and heard, next thing I know he's asking me who did what. After that they rushed me through high school and sent me to college to learn some law. Before I know it I'm carrying a Marshal's badge and that old friend of the Colonels is my new boss. Hell I was just a knocked kneed kid of seventeen, wet as hell behind the ears, and there I was carrying a buzzer and a couple of forty-fives."

"I can't imagine you as ever being knocked kneed," she said touching his arm. "I can imagine you looked pretty impressive carrying those forty-fives and sporting that badge."

"All the young girls in the neighborhood seemed to think so at least," he smiled as he remembered.

"Something tells me that you remember the girls more than you remember anything else."

"You're the only things worth remembering," he chuckled.

"So where did the money come from?" she asked smiling at what he'd said.

"It always comes down to the money doesn't it?" he laughed. "It comes from the women of the family, starting way back when. Before you ask, there's seven of us all together two girls and five boys. My youngest sister just turned twenty I have no idea what she's doing. Quite frankly I'm not sure she even knows. My older sister married a Senator. Three of my brothers followed family tradition joining the Marines and marrying women with money. We lost one of them in the war though. The youngest, well he just turned eighteen and he's off to Annapolis next term. They've all but given up hope that I'll ever get married. Too cynical they say, maybe their right."

"When did you leave the Marshal Service?"

"During that nasty little dry spell," he told her taking a sip from his flask. "I decided that I couldn't keep breaking a law I was supposed to enforce. Oh I still did some work for them and the Bureau, they tried to overlook my drinking and I tried to overlook the idiocy of it all. The only good thing that came out of that nasty little dry spell is that my taste in hooch improved. I still work cases for them both on occasion. They want me to come back full time now that the dry spell is over, but I like it better this way. I work what I want, and when I want to work. They pay me when I work for them and I get to keep my Marshal buzzer."

He sipped from his flask and chain smoked for the rest of the drive attempting to keep the pain at bay. While she laid her head on his shoulder and napped.

He nudged her awake when they reached the club. It was still way too early for it to be open not that he cared, he wasn't there for cocktails anyway. Telling Johnny to wait, he walked past the club, heading straight for the cabins that stood just inside the trees. Andrea didn't question him as she kept close. Finding the one he was looking for he knocked hard on the door. The windows rattled as his knuckles raked the door. After a minute of knocking a sleepy voice asked what they wanted.

"I brought you something from Tuna," Dawson said disguising his voice.

"Yeah okay just a minute,"

He pulled one of the automatics and waited for them to open the door. she was about to do the same but he shook his head pushed her to where she would be the first thing they saw when they opened the door.

"He's got a lot of nerve sending someone out here this time of day," they said as they opened the door in their underwear. "Oh, umm hello and welcome to Little Johnnies Hideaway Club and Motor Cabins."

Calvin "Stretch" Jones took a step out the door to let her in and Dawson shoved the barrel of his gun in his ribs.

"Nice and easy now," he told him, "back inside."

The cabin was small with a bed toward the back and a couple of overstuffed chairs against the wall. A small counter with a sink, an icebox, a hot plate, and a night stand rounded out the rest of the furnishings.

"I should have known you weren't from Tuna," he cursed at him. "Damn you Dawson what do you want from me this time. I'm clean now you've got nothin' on me."

"Oh, I don't know," he returned looking at his arms. "You're arms are starting to look like the Union Pacific Railway. I imagine I could have a narcotics team out here and you'd be sittin in the big house again within a couple of hours."

Stretch grabbed a shirt and pulled it on.

"Those are old," he returned beginning to get nervous. "I've been straight for a year or more now."

"Really then I suppose you won't need this kit over here," Andrea chimed in pointing the syringe and spoon on his nightstand.

"I had a girl over she must have left it behind."

"Okay Stretch I'll believe you," Dawson said sitting in one of the kitchen chairs. "You can do whatever you want. I'm not here for you anyway. I'm looking for a couple of Joey's typists, the ones that shot up Thirty-Eighth Street a couple of nights back."

Still nervous but less so now that he knew that he wasn't looking for him. Just the same he told him that he didn't know what he was talking about.

Dawson rubbed his chin, looked at Stretch and then to Andrea.

"I know they're out here, you know they're out here. Hell even Mikey 'The Nose' knows they are out here and he's sitting in the can." He said standing up and returning his gun to his holster. "All you need to do is just come clean and tell me which one of these shacks their hiding in."

"They'll come here and kill me after you leave," he breathed a little easier as he watched him putting away his gun.

He told him that it wouldn't be a problem, that he'd put it all on 'The Nose'.

"Really, you'd do that," he returned seeing his out.

"What do I care," he smiled hoping that he was about to break. "Mikey and me go way back I'm sure he won't mind."

He could see the wheels turning in his head as he thought about it. There was no way that he wanted to kick the needle in the pen again. The last time nearly killed him.

"The three of them are down in the cottages, they're in number five it's away from the others so that no one see's who comes or goes. Joey is the only one that uses it unless he needs to hide any of the boys out for a while." He began as if he were letting a weight off his chest and the farther off it got the easier and faster he spoke. "They aren't alone though they got girlfriends with them. Some of Tuna's girls that ain't too picky if you know what I mean."

"Look at that," he told him. "I didn't even need to sock you around."

"Thanks for that Dawson," he said. "My nose still hurts sometimes when it rains."

"I'm not sorry to hear that," he told him fighting back his laughter. "Then I know that you're not going to fuss when I tie you up for now."

Andrea grabbed a few ties from a drawer and tied his hands together as Dawson tied his feet. Flopping him on the bed when they finished they rolled him up in the sheets making him nice and snug. For good measure he wrapped a bar of soap in a washcloth and stuffed it in his mouth.

"I hope you won't hold this against me," he added as he made sure it wasn't going anywhere. "I can't have you yelling out either. If I have time I'll stop on my way out and untie you. If not I'll send someone else to do it."

Stretch nodded as the two left the cabin.

They stopped outside of cottage five and looked around.

"I don't suppose there's any way I can get you to wait outside while I go in?"

She shook her head no telling him that she hadn't just come for the scenery. That's when he told her that he'd only let her come along to humor her.

"I knew that," she smiled, "I wasn't going to let you know that I knew though. I'll be good I promise, just tell me what to do."

Pulling out his automatics he spun a muzzle on each of them. Handing her one they made their way up to the cottage window. Looking in he saw all six of them in the living room with a bunch of empty champagne and liquor bottles scattered around. He jerked his thumb at the window and she looked in.

"Looks like it was quite a party," she whispered as she looked over the pile of naked and half naked men and women.

Nodding in agreement he pointed toward the door.

Once inside Dawson pulled up a wooden chair that was against the wall and sat down. Taking a long pull from his flask, he lit a cigarette as he contemplated which of the passed out bodies he was going to try to shake loose first. Andrea grabbed a chair from the kitchen and sat on the other side of the pile. Reaching over he knocked an empty bottle from the end table. It crashed against the wood floor, bouncing a few times before rolling away. The noise didn't wake them although one or two, it was pretty hard to tell for sure, did move a little. Andrea smiled and proceeded to knock four more off their perch and onto the floor. Two of the bottles smashed into each other and broke as they hit. Even that didn't seem to create enough movement to tell where one began and another ended for sure. Stubbing out his cigarette he reached out with his foot and kicked hard at the head of Eddie 'Two Time' Haggerty.

"Hello Eddie," he said as his eyes fluttered open. "Not moving very fast this morning. Too much wine women and song I take it. Can't say that I'm not surprise to see you here. Last time I saw you weren't you were on your way to the Texas state pen."

He tried to shake himself loose from the pile but it didn't work very well. Eddie told him in no uncertain terms just what he could do to himself.

"Now Eddie," he chided, "is that any way to speak in front of a lady?"

"These ain't ladies," he laughed poking one of the girl's bottoms.

He pointed to Andrea and told him that he should apologize to her.

"Why would I want to do that," he laughed again. "If she hangs out with you for long she'll hear it all sooner or later. So's she might as well get used to it now."

Reaching down and grabbing him by his ear he pulled him reluctantly out of the pile. As he did so they came to one by one.

"What the hell Dawson you ain't got no right to do that."

"I wanted to take you back to your school days Eddie, when

you were supposed to have learned something."

The girls looked confused as they rose from the floor. When Andrea stood up leveling the forty-five at them they seemed to understand what was going on.

"Never mind being modest now ladies," she told them as they tried to cover themselves. "Just have a seat on the couch and maybe this won't take too long."

Betty wasn't having any of it as she stepped toward her.

"To hell with you b…" was all she could get out before Andrea laid the barrel of the automatic hard to the side of her head. Betty hit the floor in heap. She asked the other two if they had anything they wanted to add before they sat down. Shifty and Stitch could only seem to watch bewildered and amazed.

"I imagine with her hang over dear, she won't know which is worse." He told her.

She smiled back at him and he could see the adrenaline running through her.

"I guess we know not to mess with her," Joe 'Shifty' Barton began. "What about you mister, you got the same?"

"All you got to do is give it a go to know for sure."

"Easy Shifty," Two Time told him. "He's got that and more trust me."

Eddie and Dawson knew each other and that was a fact that neither would question. Eddie had watched him take on three guys by himself when Dawson had caught them trying to rob a bank in Texas. Eddie had gone out to visit his sister when he'd run into the three of them. One of them was living with his sister and asked if he wanted to help out. Dawson was at the bank waiting for them though and they didn't get far enough to call it robbery only attempted robbery. The other three ended up dead and he ended up getting a year in a Texas prison for his troubles.

"I don't think he can take all of us by himself," Stitch spoke up finally.

"Probably not, but I think that between the three of us we shouldn't have any trouble." Dawson told them pointing back and forth between Andrea and him.

"I thought I was the stupid one," Hope laughed from the couch. "There are only two of you"

"You're forgetting Mr. Colt," he said waving the forty-five back and forth. "Suppose we get down to business shall we?"

"Whatever you think you want to do," Two Time said growing tired of it all.

"Why don't you tell me why you boys shot up the pawnshop on Thirty-Eighth Street the other night?"

"Who says we did that, we was here all night," Shifty said folding his arms and becoming indignant. "Just ask the girls here they'll tell ya if you don't believe us."

"How do you think I found you out here?"

"Ain't nobody knows we was out here," Two Time said starting to lose his patience.

"Tuna knows you're out here," he returned.

"Joey wouldn't tell you where we was no matter what you did to him."

"That may be, but if Tuna knows something then you know that everyone else that works for him knows too."

"What," Shifty looked at him a bit puzzled.

"Never mind who told me just answer the question." He lit a cigarette as he spoke waiting for them to answer.

"What's it to you anyway?"

"Up until yesterday it didn't matter to me," he said and then told Andrea to find something to tie them up with. "Then someone took a couple of shots at me and that made me interested in why you boys did it."

"They give you the need for those stiches on your forehead."

He nodded.

"Shame they weren't a better shot," Stitch returned.

"Yeah, lucky for you I'd say," Dawson told him.

"How's that?" Stitch asked.

"Because Pop, the man that ran the pawnshop, is dead from lead poisoning. I'd say sometime today you're going to get a visit from Abrams and his boys and be charged with his murder."

"It'll never stick," Linda said.

"Maybe not, but then again I was on the street too and I saw you boys there. You of all people know what weight that'll carry with any Judge, right Eddie."

Eddie nodded his head knowing exactly what his word would do for them.

"Whaddya want," he said finally as it sank in.

"I want you to tell me why you shot up the street."

"You know why," he replied. "Joeys been tryin to get them to pay up, you know protection. So he sent us there to persuade them."

"Shut up Eddie you'll have us all in the chair for killing that guy." Stitch raised his fist and kicked at him.

Dawson told him that using that fist wouldn't be the best idea he had that morning.

"Pop wasn't supposed to be there." Two Time began again after Dawson told him to go ahead. "Joey said he had it arranged that no one would be in any of the shops."

"Did you know there was supposed to have been a street party that night?"

"No, we wouldn't have done it if there had been a party on the street. Joey didn't want anyone to get hurt, at least not yet."

"What about Sally Masters?"

"Who, Sally Masters I don't think I know any Sally Masters."

He looked at them and believed that they didn't know that name at least.

"How about Carolyn Walsh?"

"Joey's old flame?"

"Yeah her, you weren't there to do anything to her were you?"

"Joey's been looking all over the city for that dame. I couldn't believe it when I seen her on the other side of the street. Soaking wet she was, white as a ghost too. I'm thinking that she thought we was there for her or at least going to come back around for her."

"Do you know who it was that Tuna arranged it with to keep everyone out of their shops?"

"You're on your own on that one Dawson," Two Time said, "But if I know you, you already have an inkling of an idea."

"The more I talk to you the less I think I know," he told him.

Andrea had found enough ties and cord from the drapes to tie them up. She was nearly finished tying up the women when he was done.

"What's Joey holding over her anyway," he asked.

"What makes you think he's got something on her?"

"I would think that any smart woman wouldn't have anything to do with Tuna. No there has to be something he's got on her."

Linda laughed leaning over whispering to Hope.

"What you laughing about?" Andrea asked her pulling on the cord she was using to tie her hands to her feet.

"Maybe you should ask Cecelia Robbins that question," Linda laughed again.

Johnny was waiting for them when they got back to the cab, but he had managed to make his phone call. He asked them if they got everything he needed. Dawson told him that they had done about as good as he had suspected. Then he asked him if he had gotten a hold of Joey. Without thinking Johnny answered yes. His eyes shot to the mirror as he realized what he'd said. But Dawson showed no sign of having heard him.

"You mean my wife," he said trying to cover up. "Yeah I caught her to let her know I might be late."

"Good, I guess we're all set then." He told him settling back in the seat. "Let's head back then, there's a little wagon out this side of the city that we can catch something to eat before we get back."

He took a long pull from his flask rubbed his forehead and then his shoulder. She talked him into taking off his overcoat and jacket then took over the ministrations on his shoulder. She asked him if the holster was bothering and told her it wasn't.

"Who's Cecelia Robbins?" she asked finally.

"Took you Ten minutes longer to ask that question than I

thought it would take you," he smiled taking another drink before telling her.

As he told her who Cecelia was he kept his eye on Johnny and where he was driving them. After a while he tapped Johnny on the shoulder and told him that the lunch wagon he wanted should only be about a mile or two further.

"There at the crossroad," he said pointing ahead.

"I don't see any food joint here," Johnny said pulling to a stop on the side of the road.

"We might be a little early," he added getting out and looking at his watch. "Here he comes now."

"Maybe we ought to get back in the city," Johnny said sounding a little worried.

"You thinking about your meter?" Andrea asked.

"Oh, no I know he's good for whatever the meter says."

"Then we'll wait."

The horse drawn wagon pulled onto the side of the road diagonally across from the cab next to a grove of trees. A boy jumped off the seat and started putting blocks under the corners of the wagon. Putting a jack under the tongue he lifted it a few inches and slid another block under each of the front corners. When he was finished he pulled a pin and gave the lead reins a shake. The horses stepped away from the wagon. Leading them back down the road the boy waved to his father who was coming out of the wagon.

Dawson told Johnny to park the car around behind the lunch wagon. When he asked why he told him it was so he could eat in the shade. He doubted that the cabbie believed him but he didn't care. With Andrea still in the car he pulled it around to where he was told to park it. Tipping his hat to cover the crease in his forehead he walked across the intersection and yelled hello.

"Dawson!" The man yelled back as he was lifting the side of the wagon.

He hurried across the road and helped him lock the poles that would keep the side up and open. The two shook hands when they were finished.

"I hope the horses aren't any indication as to the quality of the meat you're using these days," Dawson laughed.

Andrea laughed too as she watched from behind them.

"I see you travel in better company these days," he said pointing to her.

"I can't say for sure if it's better," Dawson returned. "But she is damn site prettier than you are brother."

He called her over and introduced her to his brother Sam.

Samuel was part of the Dawson family tradition of Marines. He was forced out after being caught in a gas attack during the war. The two had worked a few cases together from time to time. Then he'd got a job in the stock market. He'd done well for himself too, that is until the market crash. When it was all over he had just enough money left to buy a small house, with a little left over to buy the lunch wagon.

"Was that little Gunny?"

"Getting big isn't he," His brother nodded

"I thought you were going to build something on this corner."

"I haven't taken the time to buy it yet,"

This in Dawson family code meant that he hadn't been able to come up with the dough.

"What about my namesake," he asked.

"He'll be along, he's learning to drive," he said. "He's bringing his mother and a few supplies from the store out with him. Damn it's good to see you."

He slapped his brother on the shoulder and Dawson nearly dropped to his knees from the pain.

"Here," he said lifting him up and looking closer at his brother. "What happened to you?"

"Just a flesh wound," he returned.

"Flesh wound hell," Andrea said before insisting on telling him everything.

As she told his brother what happened, Dawson drank the last of the first flask. Looking around in back of the wagon he found Johnny lying against his door snoring softly. With help from the second flask the intense pain in his shoulder began to subside returning to the more manageable steady throb. As Andrea continued to tell what happened, a few of his regular customers stopped causing her to pause in telling the story and making it seem much longer.

"Never mind all that," he told her. "He doesn't care about that. Just tell him I was hit side the head and in shoulder by person or persons yet unknown. Leave it to a woman to make a book out of short story."

Sam laughed and told them that they may as well sit down and have something to eat. After telling him that was precisely what they had in mind they stepped up onto the side of the wagon. Sitting down on stools that swung out from under a counter on the side Andrea looked over the wagon and told him that it was a pretty clever set up.

"Designed it myself," Sam added beaming with pride as he showed her some of the best features of the wagon.

A few minutes later Johnny came around from the back and asked them what was taking them so long.

"You looked like you needed the sleep," she told him.

"You got any coffee on this thing?" he asked and was immediately handed a cup.

Dawson kept one eye on the road and one eye on the cabbie.

"You look familiar," Sam said looking hard at Johnny.

"I should you and your brother sent me up river about nine years ago."

"Johnny Cohen," he returned recognizing the man finally.

"Didn't you promise to pay us both back for putting you there?"

"Aw, I didn't mean nothin' by it, you know how it is," he said a little sheepishly. "You get mad at everyone but yourself for what you done when you get caught. Nah, I don't hold no grudge anymore."

As he set burgers in front of the three of them two black sedans went speeding through the intersection. Dawson took a bite of his burger told them all that they had better get moving. Sam was confused at first, but caught on as he noticed the cars going up the road and out of site.

"You tell Annie I'll be back once I get this figured out," he told him.

"She'll be sorry she missed you and what do you want me to tell ..."

"Eh, no need to say that name," he said pulling an envelope out of his jacket pocket. "Poor kid being saddled with a name like that. I was hoping that once I was dead there wouldn't have to be another kid hung about the neck with that name. Anyway, next time I come I want to see something built on this corner."

He slid the envelope across the counter and told him that he'd see him soon enough.

Sam picked up the envelope and watched them drive off before opening it.

"You son of a ...," he smiled as he notice that in the envelope was a deed to all four corner lots at that intersection.

With it was a note that read simply: Sound Business Investment.

Johnny started speeding up as he got closer to the city. His eyes were constantly searching the road for something.

"You missed Tuna," Dawson said finally, "You might as well slow down."

"I don't know what you're talking about," he returned.

However, he did slow down, but he didn't stop searching. It was as if he were waiting for something to happen or looking for a place for it to happen in. Leaning over Dawson whispered in Andrea's ear. Nodding her head she offered to rub his shoulder again.

"You read my mind," he replied taking off his jacket and dropping his holsters across his lap.

Keeping at least one hand wrapped around the butt end of his automatics he let her rub his shoulder.

Five minutes later the cab slowed down and pulled onto a narrow dirt side road. As it stopped Dawson had his automatics leveled at Johnny.

"Get out," Johnny yelled turning around in the seat with his own automatic pointed at them. "I wouldn't try it Dawson she'll be dead before you get me."

He slid out of the driver's seat and opened the back door. With Dawson's hands full of the forty-fives Johnny Cohen knew what would happen if he took his eyes off him. As she slid out first her hand came up with one of her thirty-two's in it. She pressed it against his chest before he knew what was happening.

"Looks like she's got the drop on ya there Johnny and you had yours out first." He said climbing out of the cab still holding his heaters. "Is this Tuna's idea, or yours."

"Joey don't have nothin' to do with this," he said taking a step back trying to get a little distance between him and her barrel.

"I find it all hard to believe," she said, "I wouldn't think you were smart enough to do this on your own. Then again it doesn't look as if it's going that well for you at the moment."

"Shut up," he yelled, swinging his gun toward her head.

She didn't wait for it to come all the way around as she rolled away from it. Dawson didn't really want to, but he knew that it was probably going to be their only chance. Taking advantage of the opportunity he shot the cab driver between the eyes.

"All from the hip," she said admiringly. "Not bad at all. You're going to have to show me how to do that someday."

He shook his head as he picked up his spent shell telling her it was all luck and that he hadn't wanted to kill him. He wasted no time in rolling Johnny on to his back and with his good arm they dragged his body into the back seat of the cab. A few minutes later the cab was on the paved road once again and headed back to the city.

"Too bad you didn't get the chance to find out who Johnny called," she said watching him drive.

"It was Tuna; those were two of his cars that went screaming through the intersection while we were back there at Sam's wagon."

"If you thought he was going to pull something like this why'd you let him drive us out there?" she asked him as they reached the city limits.

"Everyone is always telling me I don't trust people and that I need to give them a chance, you know the whole benefit of the doubt thing. Besides you looked like you needed a little more excitement."

She laughed as they made their way through the city streets.

"I gotta tell ya it doesn't surprise me one bit, you showin up here with a body like this." Abrams added after they told him what had happened.

He had one of the uniformed officers take the body down to the morgue and return the cab when they were through with it.

"Anything to get out of paying the fare eh Dawson," Tiny said to him sticking his head around the corner.

"Just what I needed," he shook his head and walked away.

"Come on, you owe me one after the other day."

"Tiny," he said turning around. "I don't owe you anything if anyone owes anyone you still owe me for nearly getting me killed. Not once not even twice, but three times, and each time you had said that you would sit on the story until I told you it was okay. And let's not forget the one you made up that nearly got me stretched by my neck. So, no, I don't owe you anything ever."

"But that was years ago," he said watching Dawson walk away.

"I'd give it up if I were you," Abrams said.

The reporter protested some more and asked him to give him something he could print.

"Sure," he said, "Johnny Cohen, ex-con and suspected hit-man died early this afternoon of lead poisoning to the brain."

"Can I put ..."

"You'd better not, or you just may end up next to Johnny, and I wouldn't say as if I would blame him." Abrams poked his finger in his chest to make the point. "Hell I am surprised you haven't beaten him to the slab."

Tiny made an audible gulp that made Benson laugh as he and Abrams walked away.

When they were gone he ran to the press room at the station and picked up the direct line to his paper.

"You're in on this one now aren't you?" Abrams asked as they walked out of the station.

"Whoever it was made it personal," he told him. "I don't like being shot at and I definitely don't like being hit."

"What's your next move?"

"I find the girl," he told him lighting a cigarette. "She invited me there for a reason I guess it's time I found out what that reason was."

"You mean you haven't been looking for until her today?"

"I figured she'd show up on her own," he said opening his flask and offering it to him. "I didn't know what she was hiding from until today. Then again I should have thought something was up when Morre told me to take care of her and to keep her safe."

"When did he tell you that?" he asked spinning around so fast that he nearly lost his balance.

"After he was shot, before Riley interrupted me. He was whispering to me when he came through the door."

"That all he said?"

"It's all I can say for sure," he added. "Riley doesn't exactly keep his presence a secret."

"I never have seen him look over anything first before saying something stupid."

The two laughed and agreed.

"I'm going to give you a helper," Abrams said. If he had said it any other way he would have been yelled at for suggesting it.

"I got me a great little helper already," he returned. "She's pretty quick at catching on too. This baby even comes with her own set of twins. Show the nice detective your twins."

"Sh…, Show what, what," Abrams stuttered as Andrea

giggled and said that she would love to show him her twins.

His eyes widened as she grabbed at the front her dress. Laughing harder she reached down and lifted her hem stopping when the two thirty-two's appeared at the top of her stockings.

"Ain't that four of the nicest …," Dawson added fighting back his laughter. "I mean aren't they two of the prettiest … I mean those are some nice heaters aren't they. Don't let's stop there baby show him your other twins too."

She giggling again, saying she'd love to.

"Dawson!" he yelled waving his arm so that Benson could see where they were standing on the street.

Piling into Abrams car they left the station behind them.

"They sure don't make these things big enough," he said shaking his second flask. "You better hurry up and get me home kid I have no intention of sobering up before I get started."

"What now?" Abrams asked when they reached his apartment.

"Now I'm going to get more booze," he said getting out. "This morning it was all about the Irish. It's afternoon now so I'm thinking maybe Kentucky or Scotland. I'll know better when I get up to the apartment and figure out what I have more of. Don't want to be running out of one particular kind."

"Across the street," the doorman said out of the corner of his mouth. "Two O'clock, he's been there a couple hours now."

Dawson thanked him pulled one of his forty-fives and pointed the man out for Abrams. Nodding and grabbing Benson the two of them walked across the street. Taking off on a run the man whistled as he rounded the corner. Dawson looked around for who the whistle was for. Up the street a Chevrolet coupe pulled out and sped after the running man.

"Why do they always gotta run," he said stepping out into the street.

It took him five shots but he managed to take out two tires. The car crashed into two others that were parked on the street.

"I wouldn't run if I were you," he said as the driver opened the door.

"You're not me," the driver said stepping out the car.

"Oh, no," he began in slow monotone as if he were bored. "Don't do that, stay in the car, keep your hands where I can see them, no stop or I will have to shoot."

Laughing he told Dawson in no uncertain terms what he could do to himself as he raised his rod. It never had a chance to bark before Dawson pulled the trigger on his stopper dropping the driver where he stood.

"They never learn," he said in the same monotone voice and shaking his head.

"That's two in one day," Abrams said coming back around the corner with the other man between him and Benson. "I'm not so sure I can square this one with the Captain. Why didn't you just shoot the heater out of his hand like they do in the movies?"

He told him that there was no need to square anything as the man was still alive.

"Besides, I have a little too much Irish in me to be trick shooting for your benefit," he added lighting a cigarette and shaking the still empty flasks one by one before picking up his brass.

Benson went over to the car and confirmed the fact that the driver was still alive.

With little effort on their part they learned that the two men were part of Joey's gang. He had sent them there to keep an eye on him hoping that he would lead them to the girl.

"What's Tuna want her for?" he asked them for the fifth time.

Their only answers were, a girl like her was only good for one thing and why else would you want a girl like that. That is until he pressed his knee into the bullet hole of the wounded one.

"This time remember that we haven't called a meat wagon for you yet," he told him after asking the question again.

"She was Doug Barnes girlfriend. He threatened to tell him what she was," he said forcing his words out between gasps of pain. "He forced her to be his mistress."

"Why?" he asked letting up a little of the pressure.

"Joey's had it in for Barnes ever since he lost his partners case and he got the chair," the driver added through his gritted teeth. "He promised to ruin him and everything he touched. He'll do and use anything he can to hold over Barnes."

"Didn't know he had a partner," he said looking at Abrams.

"Back when Joey was just a little hood in training," he told him. "They robbed a payroll. It wasn't very much maybe a grand or a little more. His partner got braggin about it and flashin a wad of dough around. When we went to bring him in and question him about it he killed a cop. Joey wasn't with him and they could never prove that he was at the robbery either."

Dawson nodded figuring out the rest.

"So it was Tuna that set him up on all those bribery and jury tampering charges."

He said that it was what they figured but they could never tie him to it.

"He was disbarred and lost his license to practice. Lives off the family money now, kind of like you." Laughing he put his arm around his friends shoulder and led him away.

They got the concierge of the building to finally call an ambulance, while Benson put in a call for a squad car to pick up the man he'd caught.

"What are we holding them on?" he asked as they walked away.

Abrams turned around and looked at the two men and thought for a second.

"Suspicion," he said finally before turning away again.

"You going to try and find her this afternoon?" he asked when they reached the elevator.

"Yes, I don't think I want to let this go much longer," he told him. "It's beginning to cut into my drinking time. I'll go out and talk to Barnes and see if he knows where she is first."

"And if he doesn't?"

"I have a few ideas," he smiled looking around for Andrea but she had already gone up to his apartment. "She was one of Cecelia's girls and they are a close knit bunch of girls."

"Don't I know it," he agreed. "She's been running girls and the odd few boys for over twenty years. Her and her girls have only ever been busted once. They busted her on a charge of prostitution, but all the DA ended up charging her for was running an illegal boarding house and selling hooch during prohibition. Even those charges were mysteriously dropped a week after they were filed."

"The old gal's client list is long and deep," he laughed, having seen the list. "There were a lot of nervous people that week, including the District Attorney."

"How do you know that?"

"I can't tell you that," he told him as the elevator door opened.

"That figures," he returned. "I need to get this cleared up. I'm going to have Benson hang around down here and go with you for the rest of the day."

"Now you know I don't need a body guard," he said starting to complain.

"I want him to drive you around, the way you been hitting your pain medication you'll be too tight to drive before too long."

"As a driver I accept him then," he told him changing his mind. "That is if they have my car ready yet."

"Afternoon Mr. Dawson," Jerry said to him as he entered the elevator.

"Good afternoon," he returned and the two chatted about the baseball scores as they went up.

Jerry was a good kid, a bit of a baseball junkie and he could tell you the scores of any game that had played the day before. It was all about sports for him. He had been the talk of the neighborhood he grew up in, spent all of his time tossing a ball or batting at one. There had even been talk of him trying out for the major leagues. That was before he lost his leg and the use of his right arm in a mob shootout. Now he was just as happy to talk sports with anyone that would listen. Dawson would always take a few minutes to talk to him about the games. With opening day having been just a few days earlier he had a lot of games to run down for him.

With the help of the doorman Benson was able to find the garage that kept Dawson's car. The mechanics had finished and were washing off the dirt and dust that had collected over the last three months since the last time it had been out. After a call to Dawson they handed over the key for the red nineteen thirty Duesenberg model J Torpedo Phaeton convertible to the rookie cop. Letting out a whistle he ran his fingertips over the still wet fenders as he admired the car.

"Have fun kid," Bert told him as he chewed on the stub of a cigar.

He whistled again as he sat in the driver's seat and caressed the steering wheel.

"They all do that the first time," Bert laughed and poked at one of his co-workers.

Changing his bandage Andrea noticed that he tore a couple of stitches and told him about it. He told her that he had felt them come loose when they were putting Johnny into the back of his cab. After promising to have it looked at later and to be more careful she put a new bandage on along with the extra padding.

"I think I need to get me a set of holsters like that," she told him as she helped him put his back on.

"Oh I don't know," he said. "I'm not sure I would want anything to take away from the scenery. There's too much there now hiding what's underneath. A little less fabric cut a little closer to the body and bang you'll have it then."

"Dawson!"

He laughed as he refilled the two flasks. Grabbing a full bottle of scotch the two made their way to the elevator.

"What's the extra bottle for?" she asked as they got on the elevator.

"The one I keep in the back seat always comes up empty after I've been out of town for any length of time. Evaporation I guess, the mechanics never seem to know what happens to it."

As Jerry talked baseball scores with Andrea on their elevator ride he ran quickly ran the case through his mind. He was beginning to get a good picture of what it was all about, all he needed now was an idea of who killed Pop.

Giving Benson the address he wanted as they got in the car; he pulled the empty bottle from its hiding spot and replaced it with the full one.

"See what I mean," he said tossing the empty to the doorman before they drove away.

"It must be awfully hot in that garage," she laughed. "I thought you had a two door coupe you drove in the city."

"Had is the optimal word there," he laughed. "It sits at the bottom of a ravine somewhere in Pennsylvania."

"Tight," she asked.

He told her no and didn't say anything more, she didn't ask either.

When they reached the address he told them to wait in the car and he went inside.

"Well I'll be an old," she cackled as she saw him coming through the door. "How long has it been? This is a personal call I hope. You know my influence doesn't stop at the city limits."

"I know how far your influence reaches," he smiled, "I have seen your list."

The two laughed and she offered him a drink.

"You do still partake don't you?"

"You know me Cecelia, never stopped," he said taking out one of his flasks. "How about you keep that bathtub swill for your clients and have some of mine."

"As I remember you have good taste, in booze anyway."

"It is a lot better than my choice in women."

"Now tell me honey what brings you to my doorstep."

"I'm looking for someone," he told her pouring her drink. "She used to work for you."

"How long ago," she asked. "You know I have get a lot of girls running in and out of here I don't always remember them all."

"From what I understand she's been out of your house for

about three or four years now."

"That's an awfully long time ago as girls go. I'm not sure how you can expect me to remember her."

"Because last year she was Tuna's mistress," he finished.

"You're the second person to ask about her in two days and the third in a week. Of course Tuna has been looking for her forever."

She asked him why he was looking for her.

"You have any ideas who she might run to if she was in trouble?" he asked not paying attention to what she'd just asked.

She told him of a few places and people that she may have gone to.

"I would add Douglas Barnes to that mix but he was just here yesterday asking about her. So I doubt she'd still be there especially after he learned about her past."

He asked her what she meant and she told him.

"Seems that Joey went out to his place the other night and threatened to bleed him a little if he insisted on taking up with her again," she added. "I'm not sure how he knew she was out there, but he knew. Barnes called me last night asking if I'd heard from her so I guess she must have left there and went to ground again."

He nodded as she spoke, lit a cigarette and polished off his drink. As he poured himself another one he asked her if there was anyone else she could think of.

"If you pour me another drink with that high class booze of yours I'll think on it."

"You drive a hard bargain," smiling he poured her another scotch and soda.

As he handed the drink to her, one of her girls walked in the room wearing a silk robe and nothing else. She bent over and whispered in her ear.

"Oh no honey, he's not here for that," she laughed. "This here is Dawson he don't need our services. At least I don't think he would anyway."

The girl sat down across from him with her knees tucked up to her chin. Cecelia told her why he was there as he poured and handed her a drink. Sitting for a minute and holding her drink she suddenly jumped up and ran out of the room telling them not to go anywhere.

"I need to work on her manners," she said as the girl ran up the stairs. "Maybe I should stop taking on such young girls, they're getting to be too much for me."

"Maybe it's time you retired," he told her

Cecelia laughed and told him that she could never retire.

"Where else would these young girls be this protected and this well cared for if I weren't here."

He conceded that she had a point and downed the rest of his drink.

"You know," she said pondering his face. "If I were twenty, twenty-five maybe thirty years younger I would throw this all away and go for you in a big way."

Dawson smiled as the girl ran back into the room and handed him a business card for 'Karen's Pick-Up Service'.

"I remember her talking about the girl you're looking for before," she told him. "Some of the girls use her to set up dates and things. She's mostly legit, answering for doctors and lawyers and whoever. Anyway the girls that answer the phones all used to be working girls if you know what I mean. She might know where she is."

He thanked her and kissed her cheek.

"If I only had the time," he added as she sat back down.

"My name's Cassie," she added blushing slightly, "and you can come back for me anytime."

"I guess I don't need to teach her much more than that do I," Cecelia laughed pounding her hands into her lap as she started to cough.

Pouring what was left in his flask into a couple of glasses he told them that he needed to be going.

"One more thing Cecelia," he said when he'd reached the front door. "If you were twenty-five, thirty years younger; I just might take ya."

"Oh, Dawson," she giggled.

He winked and closed the door behind him.

Settling into the back seat he thought for a few minutes before telling Benson where they needed to go next.

"Did you find out anything?" She asked as they pulled away from the house.

He told her yes, but not where she might be hiding for sure.

"I know a few places that she might be and a lot of places that she probably isn't," he said as he placed the now empty flask in with the full bottle of scotch. More importantly I have a few places where we can start."

"Wasn't that just …?" she asked somewhat surprised that it was empty already.

"Don't get excited," he said closing the hiding place. "I had help."

"There's a car following us," Benson called from the front. "You want I should lose him?"

He smiled hoping to be able to open it up a little and see if what he'd heard about the car was true.

"Nah," he told him. "I suspect we'll have to deal with whoever it is soon or later. Might's well let them make their move, so just make believe they aren't there for now, but keep an eye on them."

However, they didn't make a move and the car didn't get any closer. As they went out of the city limits the car fell back even further. Twenty minutes later they pulled through the gate of the Barnes estate.

"I've wanted to call you," he said as he greeted them. "I need you to find her again."

"It was dumb luck I found her the first time," he told him again for the hundredth time. "She came in where I was getting drunk or was it that I went in drunk to where she was. Either way it was nothing but pure luck on my part."

"You did find out she was living under a different name."

"But if I'd known she had been Tuna's mistress I might have

found her faster."

He seemed upset that he knew about her past but didn't say anything to let him know. He asked him what he was doing there and he told him that he'd come looking for her.

"I think she's the key to the whole thing that happened on Thirty-Eighth Street the other night," he began. "I also think that she's the one that invited me to be there."

He told them that she'd called him that night and that he had sent Mickey for her.

"Do you have any idea who told Tuna she was here?"

"Not one," he answered shaking his head. "I can only imagine where you found out Tuna had been here."

"Don't imagine," he said. "Cecelia told me she also told me you were there asking about her."

He admitted that he had been there, and that he had asked about her. He also told him that he had thought she was still at his place at the time.

"I called her later when I found out she wasn't here. I don't suppose she told you that."

He told him that she had.

"You can't be thinking of her for the murder of that pawnbroker," he said suddenly.

"Can't say for sure," he told him. "Does she own a thirty-eight?"

"Yes," he lowered his head as he answered, "but she couldn't have ...."

"We all do things we couldn't do when we absolutely have to or when we think there's no other way," Andrea added. "It's only a matter of timing and how desperate we are."

"For all I know," Dawson continued. "She could have shot him then you could have gone to the hospital and pushed the pillow in his face."

"But we're old friends," he said nearly stuttering. "You can't be seriously thinking anything like that."

"I did a few jobs for you, but old friends we ain't," he added as he made his way toward the door. "If there was one thing about me that you should have learned it's that I don't trust anyone, especially when it comes to murder."

Back in the car Benson told him that the car that had been following them was driving up and down the road and that Mickey had gone out to get a better look at it. They met him at the gate and asked if he recognized it or who was in it.

"I don't know who they are," he said looking over his shoulder one more time to see if the car was going by again. "But they're dressed as cops. Two uniforms driving a regular car is a little unusual don't you think Officer Benson."

Benson told them that it was. Dawson thanked the big man as they drove away.

"He scared the bejesus out of me," Benson said when they were out on the road again. "I thought he was from the car that's following us. I kept thinking I was dead for sure until he told me he was the chauffeur and wanted to know if I needed anything to drink or eat. When I finally got my heart back to beating normal, I told him who I was and about the car that had followed us out."

Dawson laughed and told him that he'd forgotten about Mickey. Then asked him if he had anyone he liked yet for the murder of the pawnbroker.

"Not really, but then I'm stuck on motive."

"Yeah that is a tough one isn't it, robbery comes to mind when you think pawnshop. It just might be but I get the feeling there's more to it than that. If I could only make a connection," just then something clicked in his head. "We need to go back."

Minutes later he was asking Mickey who had been there the night Tuna showed up.

"Doesn't he usually hire entertainment?" he asked after he told him who the guests were. "Last party I was at he'd hired some string quartet or something."

"Usually yeah," he replied. "Only this was short notice and all he could get was a piano player. He brought a girl singer with him."

You don't happen to know their names or where they were

from do you?"

"I don't remember his name but seems to me he said that he normally played in a little dive called Mike's Place."

"Jimmy," he sighed, "and the girl was a brunette looker with a helluva swing to her step."

"Maria," Mickey smiled, "Yeah, Cook caught me looking at her and I got in all kinds of trouble."

"I get the feeling that she's more trouble than either of us can imagine."

The big man nodded remembering what Cook had said to him that night.

"Do you know if either of them used the phone while they were out here?"

He told them that Cook had found her on the phone twice arguing with whoever it was on the other end.

"She kept telling them where she was and that she had to talk to him or something like that. Cook gets a little excited and doesn't always remember all the details."

"That's a problem a lot of women have when they get around you I'm sure," he laughed.

Thanking him again they headed back to the city. It wasn't long before they picked up their tail again.

"I'm going to assume for now that Abrams put them there." Benson told them. "You know keeping an eye on the rookie making sure he can handle himself."

Dawson didn't agree with him, but he didn't disagree either. The thought that they were sent by Abrams seemed to calm him and Andrea, and that was good enough for now. It was a little early when they pulled up in front of Mike's Place, but the door was open and he went inside leaving the others in the car. Jimmy was there working out a new number with Maria just as he figured they would be. There were also a few others running around cleaning and setting up for the night.

When he saw him Jimmy kept playing and jerked his head for him to come over.

"How long have you been workin for Tuna?" he asked

looking at Jimmy when he'd finished the number.

"You know Tuna and I don't get along," he said getting mad at his old friend. "You and me we go way back. You of all people should remember what he did to me."

He did but he didn't let on that he remembered. With his back to the girl he winked at him, slapped him across the face and called him a liar. Jimmy caught on too late to react as the slap connected and his cigarette flew from his lips. Pulling one of his pistols from its holster he slowly and deliberately spun a muzzle on the end of it.

"Why did you call him up and tell him that the girl was out at Barnes' house?" he asked shaking him. "What's he want with the girl?"

"I tell ya I don't know anything about it," Jimmy pleaded.

Grabbing him by the front of his shirt with his right hand he shoved his pistol under his chin with his left.

"You know what comes next if you don't tell me what I want to know," he yelled.

Everyone in the place was watching as he dragged the piano player off his stool, tossing him onto the stage.

"I'm going to give you one more chance," he nodded yelling again.

Jimmy turned his head and Dawson covered the piano player's ear as he fired the gun into the stage floor. Everything stopped as the echo of the muffled shot rang through the club.

"You killed him," she screamed "Why did you have to kill him he didn't do anything."

Dawson stood up, turned around and looked at her with the gun still in his hand.

"Oh, Jimmy," she sobbed dropping to her knees next to him.

"I didn't think, I didn't mean to get you killed."

Looking back up at him she began screaming at him.

"I did it," she yelled slamming her fists into her thighs. "I dropped the nickel on that floozy. I called Joey, I did it not Jimmy, me."

"I know," he said calmly. "You can get up now Jimmy."

"You're a ba..." she cried coming at him.

"We'll have none of that," he interrupted her.

Holding her with one hand he shoved her down into one of the chairs on the side of the small stage.

"You could have just asked me," she added clenching her teeth as she fell into it.

"You would have just lied to me like you did the other day," he said. "You were quite convincing, I nearly bought into it."

She sneered at him and he could see the contempt in her eyes.

"I had you wrapped around my finger that day, and you know it," she said nearly spitting the words as she talked. "Please sir, help me find my sister. I even had Jimmy running around like a little puppy trying to make me happy in helping me find my poor sweet sister. Joey knew that you'd do whatever favor Jimmy asked you to do."

"So everything was just lie then," Jimmy said. "All those words were just so you could use me. Telling me that you loved me all of it just lies."

Tears streamed down her face and she couldn't look at him even though he tried to force her.

"Tell me what Tuna want's with her?" he asked her, pushing Jimmy away.

She looked up at him and smiled through her tears and told him what he could do to himself.

"Since I can't get you to talk you can tell Tuna that I'll come and ask him myself," he told her and turned away. "I'm sorry Jimmy, but I have to say that for a piano player you gave quite the performance. Perhaps you need to rethink your acting career."

He caught site of Benny on his way out the door. Waving his hat at him he told him to save him a table for three for later that night.

"I hear your singer is feeling under the weather. I hope that she's better by then," he said as he reached the door. "Maybe you should just find a better one to take her place."

Dawson was out the door before anyone had a chance to ask him anything.

"What's going on here?" Benny asked confused, looking around the club.

Back in the car Benson didn't wait for him to be told where they were headed next. Immediately pulling away from the curb, he caught the car that had been following them off guard. It had circled the block and wasn't quite back around when they pulled away.

"I don't think those two were sent by Abrams," he said as he pulled away.

He asked him how he figured it out.

While you were inside I walked back toward them," he told him as he drove. "I didn't get a good look but I am sure they knew who I was because the one on the passenger side pointed at me and they took off hiding their faces."

"And what were you doing?" he asked turning to Andrea.

She hesitated and looked at the floor. Reaching over he lifted her chin with one finger and turned her head toward him. He asked her again she only smiled and batted her eyes. Wrinkling his forehead he tried to give her his funniest mean look.

"You promise you won't get angry," she said finally holding back her laughter.

"I make no such promises to bad girls."

"In that case I don't think I will tell you."

"If that's the way it's going to be." Reaching across her and grabbing her left arm he began pulling her face down across his lap. "You'll just get the spanking now that bad girls deserve."

"Okay, okay," she laughed, pulling herself away from him. "I was watching you from the front door of Mike's."

"That explains the pale look about you when I got in."

"I really thought you shot him," she added shaking her head.

He told her that he'd meant to make it look that way. Then he reached up and handed Benson the card Cassie had given him.

"Do you think you can use your influence and find out where that place is?"

The kid nodded saying he could call the station and find out easy enough.

"What are you waiting for?"

He pulled the car over on the next street corner with a police call box on it. Dawson told her to lay down on the floor of the car and wait for them. She nodded her head pulling her twin thirty-two's. He followed the rookie cop to the call box standing nearby looking around for the car that was following them. He told him that while he was at it he might as well ask Abrams if he had sent along the babysitters.

"You never did think they were from him did you?" he asked as he waited to be connected to his Captain.

He shook his head in answer hoping that he was wrong, but he knew there was little chance of that. He watched as the coupe that was following them went by. It took him a second to realize it was the right car. By the time he did there was no way for him to tell who was in it. A few minutes later the car pulled in to the curb at the opposite corner from them. He told him to stay on the line with the station and to have them send a patrol car just in case.

"When you get all the answers give me a wave, but stay on the line," he added. "I'm going to go for a short walk."

Ducking around the corner he turned up the alley making his way to the other end.

Ten minutes later he watched Benson wave his hand in the air. Pulling the still muzzled forty-five out of its holster he tapped the shoulder of uniformed officer on the passenger side of the coupe.

"Hello boys," he said when he had their attention. "Why don't you tell me why it is that you find yourselves following me around this afternoon?"

"Easy sport," the driver said, shifting in his seat. "We got orders to be here."

"Maybe you can tell me who gave that order."

"Abrams sent us to keep an eye on you."

As he told them that he was canceling their orders he fired a shot into the car's front and rear tire.

"You can tell Abrams that he can send me the bill for the new tires."

A second later a patrol car pulled alongside the coupe and Abrams stepped out of the back seat. He looked at the two uniforms in the car then over at Dawson telling him that he didn't send them.

"They're all yours then," he told him, picking up his brass.

"And you can tell them that I won't be paying for the new tires."

"Don't you want to know who sent them?" he asked him as he headed up the street to his car.

"They won't tell you the truth. You're just going to be wasting your time," he told him over his shoulder. "Besides if Tuna didn't send them, and they really do belong to you then there's nothing I can do about it."

When he reached the car again Benson was already looking over a street map trying to figure out how to get to their next stop. Within twenty minutes they were pulling up in front of the four story walk up that belonged to Karen Page.

"Are you sure you got the right address?" she asked him.

"Only one way to find out for sure," he said opening the door. "You wanna come with me this time so that you don't have to sneak around behind me?"

She smiled and nodded as the two stepped out of the car.

Telling Benson to keep his eye on things they headed up the steps to the building. They were met at the door by one of Karen's boys who recognized Dawson from a speakeasy he used to work at.

"Mr. Dawson," he said taking his hand. "It's been a while. Still gumshoeing?"

"Who me," he said innocently. "Never worked a day in my life and you can't prove a thing."

The big man laughed and agreed with him.

"Henry," he added reminding him of who he was. "I used to work at Sandy Redlan's speak on eighty-fifth."

"That's right," he returned half remembering. "How is the old gal these days, do you see her?"

"She moved to Arizona for her health," he answered.

"What's wrong with her?"

"She doesn't want to get lead poisoning from Joey Tuna."

"Then it's for good health."

The two laughed.

"I'm sure I don't really want to know why you're here," he told him putting his hand on his shoulder.

"I'm looking for a girl," he said smiling hoping that he wouldn't have to get hurt by him.

"This girl," he asked, "she in any kind of trouble?"

"The law doesn't want her if that's what you mean," he lied but only a little. "But I am pretty sure she's on Tuna's list of problems."

Henry nodded his head knowing exactly what that could mean.

"So this girl you're looking for might wind up with a little lead poisoning of her own if you can't find her in time?" he asked while trying to decide if he should let them go upstairs. "Can you promise me that you aren't here to get this girl arrested?"

He told him that he could. He was still sure that she hadn't been the one that shot and later killed Pop so at least it hadn't completely been a lie. Although he couldn't say for sure if she may or may not have been the one to shoot him.

"Wait here," he said finally going to an intercom by the stairs.

They couldn't hear what he was saying but when he came back he shook his hand again and told him that Karen would see them.

"Top floor," he said pointing up the stairs. "Cocktail hour just started fifteen minutes ago."

"Well," Dawson said starting up the stairs. "We better hurry then."

"Yes you wouldn't want to miss out on any drinking being

done," Andrea added.

"You'll do," he laughed taking her arm.

Cocktail hour was in full swing when they reached the door and were let in by another of Karen's security boys. He didn't have to imagine the damage the two could inflict if needed. He'd seen Henry's handy work before.

"Good afternoon Mr. Dawson," the maid said coming up to him. "Shall I take your hat and coat?"

He told her that he didn't think he'd be staying very long.

"That's alright honey," she added rubbing his arm. "I'll take good care of it and not let it get too far away."

He gave in, handing his coat over to her.

"How about you sweetie," she said turning to Andrea. "Can I take your hat and coat as long as I'm here."

She agreed and the girl helped her a little more than Andrea was ready for as she ran her hands over her waist and around her bottom.

"Mistress will be along soon," she said before disappearing.

"I guess I got my thrill for the day," she giggled as the girl walked away.

Chuckling they both shrugged their shoulders and began to look for Karen. Since they had no description of her they had nowhere to start. With the population of the room being nearly two women for every man it wasn't going to be an easy find.

Dawson recognized many of the men and even a few of the women. Judge Steven Brandt was huddled in the corner with a couple of lawyers whose names he couldn't remember. Brandt was a federal district court Judge. He'd never married however there were several rumors as to why. Although by the attention he was paying to two of the girls near him one would never come to the conclusion that any of those rumors were true.

"Dawson," the Judge called waving him over, "Come here and introduce me to the beauty that drapes your arm."

Not wanting to offend the influential Judge he did just that.

"Bond," he thought for a second. "Yes I know your family, Porter and Clara unless I'm mistaken."

She told him that he wasn't and that she was surprised that she had not met him before now.

"I have not seen them for years," he said while continuing to caress the half-naked women near him. "I hope that they are well."

"Yes," she returned, "quite well I'll tell them that you asked of them."

"Just don't tell them where you saw me," he chided before turning to the men nearby. "Gentlemen you should meet her mother. Absolutely gorgeous with the finest body a woman could possess. How I envied her father when he married her."

Andrea blushed as he talked of her mother.

"Tell me Dawson does the apple fall far from the tree?" he asked nodding his head toward her.

"I can't say anything about the tree, as I have never met her," he returned. "As for the apple, well you can imagine."

"Yes I can old boy, yes I can," smiling, he absently licked his lips. "Tell me what brings you to this marvelous house of fun?"

He told him that he was there to ask Karen a few questions. Keeping from the Judge what it was about.

"Although," he admitted, "I don't know what she looks like."

The Judge chuckled and asked one of the girls if they knew where she was. One of the ones he was caressing lifted her head and looked around the room.

"There," she said pointing before happily settling back down to where she was.

Karen was coming through the door when they turned to look for her. Following close behind her was Abbey, formerly known as Sally. Dropping her friends hand she froze when she saw him standing in the middle of the room. Turning Karen grabbed her hand and pulled her along.

"Cecelia called me," she began when she reached him. "Told me that if I knew where she was I should tell you and that it would be all right."

He nodded reaching for her hand.

"She's safe with us," he said shaking Karen's hand.

"Good I don't need no trouble from you or the cops," she added. "I heard you're a G-man or were one anyway. Cecelia trusts you and that's good enough for me. She says you and her go way back."

He tilted his head and waggled his hands and told her they kind of went way back.

"You can talk in here," she said leading them to what looked like an office.

After she left he pulled the wrinkled note from his pocket.

"Want to tell me what this was all about?" he asked her as she looked at the note.

She didn't say anything for a minute. Sitting there she kept looking at each of them and then back at the note.

"I trust her," he told her finally. "She tells anyone what she knows she won't live long enough to profit from it."

Abbey smiled as Andrea's eyes got big and appeared to bug out of her head.

"Geez Dawson I didn't think you could be that way," she said as her eyes slowly got smaller.

"Pop suggested I talk to you," she said finally. "He said that you could help me."

"Did you see who shot him?"

"Yeah it was Stitch and Two Time, a couple of Joey's boys."

Dawson shook his head and then told her that they couldn't have.

"Pop had thirty-eights in him. The typewriters those boys use take forty-fives."

"Did you see anyone else?" Andrea asked impatiently.

"You mean besides him," she answered pointing a finger at him, "No, just those three and you Dawson."

"Why didn't you come over and talk to me when I saw you walking across the street?"

"I was afraid to be seen with you," she said nervously. "I was expecting the big street party for that neighborhood kid, Willy something or other. I figured it would be better to talk to you in a crowd, harder to be seen that way."

He agreed and told her that it was the smart thing to do if she was afraid.

"Does Tuna want to kill you?"

"Kill me or use me," she said. "I don't think he cares which. Even though…"

She stopped and looked away from them.

"Even though he wants to use your past to bleed your boyfriend Douglas Barnes for whatever he can get."

She turned her head back to him quickly surprised that he would know about that.

"You must have a lot on him," Andrea added.

"I've known him a long time," she said, "since before I started in the business. He wasn't much more than a punk hood with dirt under his fingernails coming around collecting protection money."

"Sounds like you could do some damage if you wanted to," He told her.

"I value my life too much," she said shaking her head. "I just want him to leave me alone and let me live my own life."

"Why don't you get us something to drink," he said turning to Andrea.

She didn't want to but did it anyway protesting the all the way out the door. When she was gone he continued asking questions.

"You knew Pop quite a while then to take his advice."

She nodded and told him that she had known him all her life.

"I grew up near there," she said. "I know everyone on that street that's been there for any length of time. I used to visit Pop from time to time. He used to tell them I was his daughter from Florida, but some of them knew he didn't have a daughter, at least not one as young as me anyway. His wife and daughter died in a hurricane in Florida when she was little, long before he moved here. He had a son too only he was killed in the Spanish war."

Does Tuna know all this," he asked.

"Nah, you're the first person I ever told this too," she said a tear forming in her eye. "Only Pop, Abraham, me and now you know I grew up there."

"Dershowitz?" he asked.

She nodded and told him that she visited the both of them from time to time.

"I worked for him from the time I was ten until I was fourteen," she said wiping her eyes for the third time. "They're the two most honest men I ever met. I never trusted anyone except those two, well before I met Douglas anyway."

"You got Pop to sell off your rocks," he began. "Were you going to go away when you had enough money?"

She shook her head no and told him that she wanted to stay in the neighborhood. Open up a shop of some sorts or maybe even take over the pawnshop for Pop.

"You know, help the kids like they do, or did rather."

"You still have the thirty-eight you got from your boyfriend?"

She hesitated to answer him thinking back on his questions and what he'd said.

"Yeah," she said finally remembering that he had said that he knew she didn't shoot Pop.

Andrea returned with their drinks just as she finished.

"What are you going to do now," he asked. "Go back to Barnes, or you want me to hide you up somewhere."

"I'm pretty sure I'm safe here," she said. "I got some money left maybe I can take up for Pop in a few months when things cool down a little."

"Tuna's still going to be around and so isn't Riley," he added.

"You don't really think you can keep either of them from finding you there. Not when Tuna's got that street wrapped up in his insurance racket do you?"

"Yes Dawson I do think I can," she smiled and downed the drink in front of her. "There's not much you can do for me now I am afraid. If you will excuse me I should be getting back, I have to get ready to answer phones."

He knew that she wasn't telling him everything. He also knew that there was no way she was going to tell him, at least not right then. When she had left the office they took a minute to finish their drinks before making their way back to the other room. Cocktail hour was quickly degrading to something with less clothing.

"Let's get out of here while we still can," he said taking her arm and going in search of the maid.

"Dawson old boy," the Judge called to them. "I hope that you two aren't leaving now that the real fun is just beginning."

Making his apologies he told the judge that they were.

"That's too bad ol' boy," he returned. "I should have liked to see about that apple, but another time perhaps. I come here every week at this time be sure to come back won't you."

"Perhaps I could speak to my mother," Andrea added hoping to change the subject away from her.

"Oh," the judge returned. "That would be just delightful. She and I used to go skinny dipping in the pond, what memories."

Andrea's eyes widened as she blushed again for the second or was it the third time that day.

Leaning in Dawson whispered in his ear.

"Yes," the judge smiled agreeing with him. "You're quite right, quite right in deed."

Judge Brandt was still nodding his head as he went back to his place in the party.

"What did you tell him," she asked.

"Now where could she be," he replied ignoring her and looking for the maid once again.

They found her right where they left her.

"It's too bad you're going now," she smiled helping her with her coat. "We're just starting to have a little fun."

She again slid her hands over her as she had done earlier.

"I can see that," he told her. "We'd like to stay and join in but we have a previous appointment that won't wait."

While helping him with his coat she was even more open with her reach than a mere rubbing of his arm.

"I'd say we both got a good thrill for the day," he told her as they went down the stairs.

"That was interesting, I can tell you that much. Wait until I see mother, she is forever telling father that I ruined her. Now I know what she meant," she laughed putting her head on his shoulder. "Stick with you and I will never be bored again."

Henry was missing from the door and back in the car Benson was slumped over the wheel. Pulling one of his forty-fives he went back inside. Andrea lifted her twin thirty-two's and headed to the car to check on Benson. Picking up the intercom he called upstairs and let them know that Henry wasn't on the door. As he hung up the receiver he noticed blood on his hand.

"He's alive," she told him running back up the steps. "I'll get a neighbor to call an ambulance. Did you find Henry yet?"

"I only had time to let them know upstairs," he said showing her the blood on his hand.

"There's more blood," she said pointing to a trail on the floor leading to the back of the building.

"You make that call and then call for Abrams," he told her following the blood. "Then get back out there and keep an eye on the kid."

She told him that she didn't know the address.

"Then call upstairs and have them call. I still want you to stay with the kid though."

Pulling his other forty five he followed the trail of blood as it led into the basement. Finding the doorman slumped over the railing at the bottom of the stairs he checked to see if he was still alive.

"Sorry, old man," he whispered to the body that used to be Henry.

He was about to go back upstairs when he heard a voice.

"The boss is disappointed with you," they said.

Then he heard another voice that sounded like Carolyn telling the man exactly what his boss could do to himself. The slap that followed was loud enough to carry through the basement.

"Where are they?" he asked her.

"They're mine," she said, "they were given to me."

There was another dull sounding slap before he figured out which direction it had come from. Finding the room he glanced in to get an idea of what was happening. He saw Carolyn sitting at the kitchen table with a bloodied nose, her dress torn and the side of her face swelling up. One man stood to her left and another stood in front of her.

"I don't think you should hit her again," he told them slipping in behind them.

The one closest to him turned first and he slammed the butt of one of his forty-fives into the side of his head. Staggering backwards the man fell to the floor in a heap.

"You have anything to add to that?" he added leveling his free automatic at the remaining intruder. "I really don't want to have to kill you. I can, it won't bother me and I won't lose sleep over it either, but I don't want to have to."

"You don't have the nut," he said smiling.

He turned toward Dawson and began to raise the baseball bat in his hand.

"Tuna doesn't have the smartest men does he," as he talked he turned both guns on the man. "It's your choice; put the bat down and live or raise it up a little more and they'll be fixing you for a Chicago overcoat in a heartbeat."

"You can't kill me," he said taking a step toward him but lowering the bat just a little.

"Like I said Tuna doesn't have the brightest people on staff. I would bet that you're not the smartest of them either."

It was then that he realized that they weren't alone anymore. Turning sideways and dropping to one knee he looked to his left to see who had come in behind him. With his head in the strike zone the intruder began to swing the bat. It didn't get far before there were three slugs in his chest and a fourth entering his head. As the bat came around in the dead man's hand he dropped to the floor and rolled away from him. Turning his attention back to the door he watched as a third man fell. Andrea stood behind the falling man with smoke leaking form the barrels of her twins.

"Yup," he sighed looking at her "You'll do all right."

"She's not dead is she?" she asked going over to Carolyn.

He shook his head telling her that she was just unconscious

"They did a number on her in a very short time though."

"Carl said there were three of them," she said talking fast. "I figured I had better come and make sure you were alright. I see I was just in time too."

"How's our boy?" he asked standing up.

She shrugged her shoulders and told him that she couldn't say for sure.

"The Judge was out there taking charge and a couple of the girls were helping him when I came down."

"I hope he's conscious enough to enjoy the view." He said running some cold water into a pitcher.

Tossing the cold water on the on the still unconscious intruder he sat in one of the chairs at the table. As the intruder came to spitting and sputtering he lit a cigarette and waited for him to stop.

"You boys didn't waste any time," he said pointing to the unconscious woman.

"Who me," he said smiling. "I was just walkin by when me and my pals heard a girl screamin. So we came to check it out next thing I know some guy clunks me over the head."

"You must be one of Tuna's smarter boys," he said laughing.

Two uniforms appeared in the door with their guns drawn, with Abrams a step behind them.

"Three in one day this must be some sort of a record for you," he said pointing to the two bodies.

"It isn't," he told him taking a long pull on his flask, "but for the record, that one's hers."

"How about the wet one, he got anything to say?" he asked as one of the uniformed officers cuffed him.

"That one claims to have been taking a walk in the park with his buddies."

"We was just helpin the dame," he said struggling against the cop. "Then this guy here burst in and just started shooting. I want him arrested for killing my pal."

"That how it went," Abrams asked.

"Yeah," the hood started again.

"Shut up," the uniform said shoving him into the door frame on the way out. "You gotta watch where you're goin'. That could leave a mark."

The officer smiled as he took hold of him again and led him out the door. Abrams told the other one to have them send the ambulance doctor when they arrived. Karen came running down the stairs and into the room. She went straight to her friend crying and telling her it was going to be all right. While she and Andrea took care of her Dawson told Abrams what had happened, including the conversation they'd had upstairs. As he was telling him, the girls helped her out and on to the street to meet the ambulance.

"She's the one that invited you there then," he said when he'd finished. "You think she was telling you the truth?"

"Yes I do, only," he paused and lit a cigarette. "Only she didn't tell me everything, but I've got a pretty good idea what she left out."

"You think you're ready to tell me who you like for the murder?"

"As soon as you tell me who you like for it."

"And here I was counting on you to solve this one for me," he laughed. "Come on let's get out of here."

When they reached the street they were just in time to see Tuna's boy being put in the back seat of a patrol car.

"When Tuna bails you out," Dawson yelled. "You tell him I'll be coming to see him."

The obscenities that came from the hoods mouth in answer could have made a sailor blush.

"I'm sorry about the blood in your car," Benson said to him when he checked on him.

"Don't worry about it kid," he said patting him on the leg. "You want me to call your wife or something?"

"I don't have a wife," he returned. "They already called my

Pop he'll be there when I get to the hospital the way I got it figured."

"How about I get the cute blonde that's hovering around and keeping an eye on you to be your nurse, would you like that?"

Benson blushed and tried not to look at the girl.

"I can do that you know," he said waving to the girl. "What's your name love?"

"Debbie-Jo" she said smiling and taking a step closer.

"Well Debbie-Jo," he smiled back at her waving her even closer. "Carl here, that's this fine strapping lad's name."

"I know," she said placing her hand on Benson's forehead. "I been talking to him and looking after him."

"Oh, you have," smiling he winked at the kid. "Moving pretty fast there aren't you kid. Anyway the kid here said that he wanted you to marry him and take care of him."

"Dawson," they both said in unison, their faces turning red.

"I think you're all set here then kid," lighting a cigarette he walked away.

"If you don't need us anymore Chester I think we'll be leaving."

"I think the maid has other ideas," Andrea added pointing to the girl.

The small girl was on her knees with her head inside the car. Another girl was busy inside it as well. They both were wiping up any blood they could find. He spotted Karen talking to her remaining security man. Telling him that it was the least she could do, she waved and bowed as if to say you're welcome.

"Can't complain about the service of this house," he smiled.

As he headed toward his car to check on their progress he noticed Riley hanging out with three other uniformed officers.

"You're a little off your beat aren't you?" he asked walking up to the four of them. "What brings you way over here?"

"I heard someone killed you," he answered. "I wanted to be in on the celebration."

"I hope you didn't order the flowers yet," he returned tossing his cigarette to the curb. "You'd be wasting your money."

"I wouldn't be so sure about that," he said before walking away from him and the three uniformed cops.

"Touchy fellow isn't he?"

"The day isn't over yet Dawson you never know what might turn up."

"Oh, just one more thing if you don't mind," he called after him ignoring his statement.

"Yeah I do mind," he said continuing to walk away.

"We can talk now or I can have Abrams haul you in when you're in your nightshirt."

"I wouldn't do that if I were you," he said coming back toward him. "Understand this Dawson, you ain't nothin' to me. I could care less who you worked for or what you did before. Now you're just a has been with a private dick buzzer. To me that means you're just like the rest of them, another bottom feeder."

Abrams noticed the commotion and walked over to the two.

"What's going on?" he asked when he got there.

"Your boy Riley was giving me a lesson in ocean hierarchy," he told him, "as to what's on the bottom tier anyway."

"I take it he doesn't think that you rank very high," he returned. "Just what are you doing here Riley? Your beat is at least fifteen blocks from here."

"I'm a cop I go where ever there are problems." Riley added stepping up to face him down. "Don't lean on me Abrams you aren't much better than he is."

"Did you guys bring him here?" he asked the other three.

They all shook their heads no and took a step back from them.

"So you're sticking your nose in where it's not supposed to be."

"I'm not going to put up with this crap. I got a beat to walk," Riley cursed at him and turned away.

"That's exactly my point Riley, that and the fact, as I said before, your beat is at least fifteen blocks away."

As Carolyn was being helped into a second ambulance a car pulled around the corner screeching its tires. Looking up the street Dawson made out the image of a Thompson being pushed out the passenger window. Yelling for everyone to take cover he ran toward the ambulance, pulling his forty-fives as he went.

The Thompson opened up and rattled off as he rolled into the gutter pulling the maid from his car with him and covering her. He was up in an instant as the car passed them and he took off running behind it. He emptied both magazines but it didn't help as the car skid around another corner two blocks away. He immediately jettisoned the empty magazines and replaced them. A minute later another car passed them as they checked to see if everyone was alright. As it passed him, he thought he noticed Eddie "Two Time" Haggerty as he slumped down in the back seat.

After Dawson told him who he'd seen in the second car, Abrams told him that for hit men they weren't very accurate. There wasn't any dead and only three wounded, two of his detectives and one of the neighbors that happened to be out in the street. None of them were seriously wounded.

"Seems everyone is alive at least," Andrea said helping Carolyn up from the sidewalk next to the Ambulance.

"Dammit," Karen yelled, "That was my best side too. You son of a, I'll get you for this."

Looking at her they saw the blood coming from her bottom.

"Make that four wounded," Abrams added holding back a laugh.

"Anyone else not going to be able to sit down for a few weeks," Dawson added, he on the other hand couldn't keep himself from laughing. "I guess calling Joey came back and bit you in the end."

"I, I didn't call Joey," she returned looking at Carolyn. "I swear I didn't honey, I promise."

Carolyn sat in the open back door of the ambulance as the doctor and driver looked after the other wounded.

Riley took Karen by the arm and whispered in her ear as he led her limping toward the ambulance.

Carolyn hadn't seen him before then, but as soon as she saw Riley she started to shake in fear. She kept pulling Andrea in front of her so that she could hide behind her. Dawson saw what was happening and went to her side blocking her further from him. Two more ambulances arrived and he steered Riley and Karen away from her toward one of them.

"How bad is it?" he asked as she limped over.

"Just grazed me really," she said lifting her skirt and showing him her bare bottom with the crease in it.

"Well that's pretty, um good," he added nodding his head. "Not bad at all."

"Glad you like it," she smiled back as she held her skirt up.

"Don't go anywhere Riley I'm not done talking to you."

"I'll go anytime I damn well want to," he replied shoving his finger into his chest and cursing.

Dawson looked down at the finger then back at its owner. Grabbing the hand before it could be removed. Twisting he pulled it down around and then up behind Riley's back. Pushing him up against the ambulance he told him that what he'd done wasn't his smartest move of the day. Abrams came running breaking the two apart.

"Keep him away from me," Riley yelled as they were pulled apart.

"I have some questions I'd like to ask him," Dawson returned calmly. "Don't let him go anywhere just yet."

Turning around he noticed bullet holes in one of the ambulances and then the ones in his car. Shaking his head he didn't look any further, walking over to it he ran his fingers over a few of the holes.

"I do so like this car," he said counting the holes. "I guess I need to have a longer talk with Tuna now."

Still shaking his head he went over to the ambulance where Andrea and Carolyn were.

"You want to tell me now what else you saw that night at the pawn shop?" he asked sitting next to her at the back of the ambulance.

She shook her head and tried to hide even further hoping that he still hadn't seen her.

"You saw Riley inside didn't you?" he said looking at her. "You saw him shoot Pop didn't you?"

She shook her head again not wanting to say one way or the other.

"Then tell me why you are hiding here if you didn't see him shoot Pop."

"He's in Joey's pocket," she whispered. "I know that he will tell Joey where I am."

"Joey already knows where you are," he told her. "You'd be better off if you told me the truth."

She told him that she was but he was sure that there was still something she wasn't telling him.

"He found out Pop was selling off your jewelry didn't he?" he asked her again. "I can imagine that he wanted to find you to get in better with Tuna. I bet Tuna wasn't happy when he found out that you took your jewelry with you when you left. I know he likes to pass that stuff on from one mistress to the next. Saves him money that way and his wife doesn't ask as many questions. I can also bet that when Riley found that out he went straight to Pop hoping to find you. I don't think Riley was thinking of turning you over to Tuna at least not right away. I think he wanted to get his hands on the rest of the Jewelry. I think he even took what you had given to Pop when he shot him."

She looked at him but didn't say a word, yet he could tell that he couldn't be any closer to the truth if he'd seen it all himself.

Abrams was still holding Riley when he approached him.

"You might as well break out your cuffs and slip them over his wrists," he said grabbing the shoulder of Riley.

"You're out of your mind," Riley yelled and told him what to do to himself. "You can't prove a thing Dawson."

Dawson laid it out for Abrams as he saw it, not forgetting to tell him of the empty boxes they'd found and the entries in Pop's ledger.

"I'm sure he even put the pillow over his head when he learned that his bullets hadn't killed him," he continued, looking between the two of them. "It was his job to make sure all the owners were out of their stores so they wouldn't be hurt when Two Time and Stitch riddled it with bullets. A dead proprietor doesn't pay off in the insurance biz. Except he saw it as a chance to steal the Jewelry that he was still holding that Sally or rather Carolyn had given him to sell. When Pop refused and fought back he shot him. Knowing that Tuna's boys were coming he didn't worry about hiding the robbery or the killing. Knowing that they would get the blame because you wouldn't think to check the slugs to see what size they were. The only thing is he didn't die and you couldn't let him come to and talk. You got lucky that he hadn't come to before you had a chance to stuff that pillow over his face. Other than someone that works there who else but a uniformed officer can walk into a hospital and not be looked at twice. The way I figure it, you had a long night of waiting for your chance to get in that room. For all I know you may have even set it up so that nurse Simon and Jacks got cozy in the linen closet."

As three of ambulances took off, the fourth was too shot up to use, Abrams stuffed the handcuffed Riley into the back of a patrol car.

With two flat tires, the same tires that had been replaced that morning and water leaking from the radiator his Duesenberg was going nowhere. After arranging to have it towed back to his garage he pulled the bottle of scotch from its hiding place and took a long drink straight from the bottle.

"Good thing I brought this with me," he said when he'd finished.

Abrams and Andrea laughed at him as he sat on the curb shaking his head complaining about his car.

"What do you mean you missed him?" Joey said slamming his fist on the desk over and over. "Do you wanna tell me again why I pay you guys, huh do you? I know I sure can't figure it out

I'll tell ya that right now. I'm waiting."

"Boss I don't know how we missed him," Stitch said pleading his case. "I poured the whole ribbon on to that street. Dawson was in the street running and shooting at us before I could get Shifty to stop so's I could reload. I had Two Time come a minute behind me in another car. By the time he went by the street was filling up and that Dawson guy was still in the street with both of his rods in his hands. I don't know how it was that he missed us. I don't see him as the type of person that misses what he shoots at."

"I ducked down so's I wouldn't be spotted," Two Time added. "So's, at least no one saw it was us anyway."

"At least no one saw it was us," he replied in a mocking voice. "Who else in this town do you think shoots up the streets like you two idiots? I'll tell you there isn't one. Do you think that the cops won't know who shot up that street? Do you really think that Abrams won't be knocking on that door any minute? If I had half a mind I would hand you both over to him."

Two Time had to laugh at his boss.

"What are you laughing at?" Joey asked angrily.

"Just what you said boss, that if you had half a mind." He laughed again only this time Stitch laughed with him. "Ain't that what your wife keeps tellin you, that you only got half a mind?"

Joey joined in their laughter except his wasn't real. Reaching into the top drawer of his desk he pulled his thirty-eight and shot them both in the shoulder.

"You shot me," the two echoed nearly in unison.

"And you're both lucky it's only in the shoulder," he said putting his gun back where it was. "Next time you guys won't be so lucky, now get out of here you're bleeding all over my furniture and brand new carpet."

The two started to complain but stopped knowing that they were very lucky indeed and it wouldn't do them any good anyway.

"You better get yourselves to the doc and get taken care of," Joey hollered at them as they left his office. "Just tell him you were cleaning each other's guns and they went off without you knowing. He'll believe that knowing what idiots you two are."

Jane had supper ready and waiting for them, as promised, by the time they got back. As they ate they told her what had happened.

"I missed all the excitement again," she pouted when they'd finished.

After a shower and a change of clothes, they found themselves seated at his table at Mike's Place. Benny was ranting about what he'd done to the stage and blaming him for making his female singer quit.

"I suggest next time you don't hire one that works for Tuna and you won't have that problem," he told him.

Benny however, wasn't as easily deterred from complaining about the afternoon as he'd hoped. Every chance he got he was standing next to their table pointing out that he no longer had a female singer. He was about to complain for the fifth time when Dawson stood up. Placing a cigarette between his lips he stared at him for nearly a minute before laughing and walking away. He was still laughing as he sat down next to Jimmy at the piano. The two laughed and talked for a minute before he stood up again and walked to the front of the small stage. When the number he was playing was finished Jimmy played a little fan fair to get every ones attention.

"Ladies and Gentlemen," Dawson began.

His appearance on stage created a ripple effect of laughter among those that knew him.

"It has been brought to my attention, on more than one occasion this evening, that I am the reason that you do not have the benefit of listening to a singer." He paused and looked around; he also took the opportunity to order another drink. "Perhaps we can rectify that little problem right now. I want to invite any of you ladies that can sing to come up and give it go. Consider it your big chance, and we the audience will let Benny know who we think he should hire. Simple right, so come on up ladies and let me see what you got under your, I mean let's hear what you can do."

There was still a little laughter coming from them, but everyone waited and watched for who would take the challenge.

"I know you don't want me to sing," he said as a waiter handed him his drink. "I will if I have to, but I have to warn you I sound like a cross between a broken fog horn and your mother's old tea kettle."

No one made a move and Jimmy began to play softly behind him.

"Well okay," he began clearing his throat. "But don't say I didn't warn you."

Jane stood up and headed toward him as Abrams came through the front door.

"Okay, okay I get it you didn't have to get the coppers involved," looking at Jane he pointed to the detective.

"I wouldn't do that darling," she said reaching the stage. "I have come to rescue you, well actually to save these fine people here from having to hear you sing."

She pulled him off the stage before climbing up.

"Believe me," she added after she had a word with Jimmy. "I did you all the biggest favor of your entire lives. He's not joking about his singing voice."

After the laughter died down again Jimmy began playing and Jane added the words.

"That's our gal," he said touching Andrea's hand.

"Did you see the late edition," Abrams said as he sat down.

"You know I don't read that trash."

"This one you should," he added flopping the paper in front of him.

'G-Man Murders Hack!'

"I suppose the Chief wants you to drag me in again," he said after reading the head line.

"You know that's Tiny's byline."

"Who else would have the nut to write it? I suppose he even used my first name."

"You mean he knows that your first name is…"

"Don't even think about saying that name," he said ordering them a drink.

"Nothing for me thanks," he told the waiter, as he set a drink in front of Dawson.

"How's the kid doing?" he asked changing the subject. The last thing he wanted to talk about was Tiny.

"He'll be fine," he said chuckling.

"What's so funny?"

"That girl from the house is there taking care of him," he said laughing. "She won't let the nurses near him without her being right there. If he's not careful she's going to nurse him right to the church altar."

"She's a pretty girl. It'll be good for him, might even make him a better cop."

"Getting married didn't make me a better cop."

"Yes, well at least you're trying."

"Isn't that Doug Barnes coming in the door?" he asked trying to ignore what he'd just said.

Dawson turned his head only to find that there wasn't anyone coming in the door. While he was distracted Abrams reached over took his drink and downed it. By the time he turned back the glass was empty and back in front of him. He looked around the table at the all glasses closing one eye and raising the eyebrow of the other he looked at Abrams and then Andrea. He shook his head and sighed saying not again. Grabbing a cigarette he put it in his mouth and lit it.

"Which one of you did it this time?" he asked waiting for the waiter. "Not going to own up to it are you."

As the waiter set his drink down he took hold of it with both hands and watched his two companions.

"Did Riley own up yet?" he asked after a minute.

"No but the lab boys are pretty sure that his gun fired the bullets into Morre." Abrams began. "They came up with some good evidence after having a look around in his apartment. He was living pretty good there too. I figure he must have been on

Joey's payroll for a while."

"That and the bribes he got from all the other crooks in the neighborhood," he added getting the bullet that had come out of his shoulder from his pocket. "I think that you'll find that this came from the same gun."

"I wouldn't doubt it if Tuna paid him a piece of the protection racket on his beat. There've been a lot of unsolved crimes in that neighborhood over the past few years."

"And Pop was just trying to protect her, the only family he had left, even though she wasn't his real daughter."

"There are just a couple of things I don't understand," Andrea interrupted. "Who told Joey that she was there, and why did they try to kill her."

"You got this one Chester?"

"Not me," he complained. "I'm still a little mystified as to a few things myself."

"Karen didn't call Tuna," Dawson started. "None of her people did really. She called Riley. He knew they were friends. I figure he leaned on her a bit on the off chance that she would get in touch with her. He was the one that called Tuna hoping to get a big payday out of it, he wanted her back, if not he at least wanted the jewelry back. He didn't bother her out at Barnes place because he figured he'd cash in by bribing him. When the word got out that she'd gone missing again all bets were off and he was out to send a message. He sent the three that shot the kid, Henry and beat up Carolyn or Sally or Donna or Abbey, or whatever she wants to call herself."

"What about the typists," Andrea asked. "Why do you figure he sent them to kill her?"

"They didn't come to kill her," he added. "They were sent to tie up the loose ends. His muscle was to finish her off after they got the jewelry from her. Riley was supposed to be outside waiting and keeping an eye out for trouble. And that's who he sent our typist friends after. I do hope that you have a more reliable officer outside her room tonight than you did Pops room. I don't think she's in the clear as far as Tuna's concerned. Once he bails out what's his name you can be sure that she'll be in for more."

"What's his name?" Andrea asked.

"Henry 'Skeez' Bascom," Abrams told them. "He's a three time loser though. He won't see daylight that doesn't come through iron bars or over a wall ever again."

After a half hour on stage Jane returned to the table to the sounds of applause.

"I hope you didn't forget about me," she said as she sat down. "You three have been huddled here forever I bet not one of you heard me singing. Where's my drink?"

"You were singing?" Dawson asked glancing at her.

"I don't know why I bother," she said hitting his arm and laughing.

"I'm sure you bother quite well darling," Andrea returned. "I remember that you sang very well in college."

"So you're a song bird from way back," he returned. "Oh, the things you hide from me. What's wrong darling don't you trust me knowing your secrets?"

Benny made his way back to the table for the first time since she had taken the stage.

"You were wonderful my dear," he said taking Jane's hand. "I couldn't have done better in replacing Maria. No thanks to your boyfriend I still need someone to replace her. You wouldn't be interested would you?"

"Yes we know I made her quit, now go away, you can't have this one."

"She's already spoken for," Andrea added.

"It seems my managers have spoken," Jane said ending what was soon to become begging by Benny.

"Alright," Benny said giving in. "But if you'll do another set in an hour I'll take care of the tables tab."

"She'll do it," Dawson said immediately calling their waiter.

He ordered a round and gave instructions for further orders.

"You'll need to repeat that order every fifteen minutes until I can't walk, then you're to repeat it every half hour. And you

Chester Abrams better get over to the hospital and get someone other than Jacks on her door and someone on the kid's door as well."

Agreeing with him Abrams said his goodbyes and left them.

"What do you mean you've been arrested," Joey said back into the phone. "You're a cop why did they arrest you."

He listened as Riley told him.

"What about the girl did they at least kill the girl before they were arrested?"

He listened again as he told him what had happened to his three men.

"All but Skeez then," he said seeming to calm down a little. "You get a chance to ask him about the jewelry?"

He paused as he listened to the answer.

"She didn't huh," he returned. "Maybe I'll have to go over there myself and do what you idiots can't."

Riley interrupted him.

"Well you're no damned good to me there," he said. "But I can't bail you out either you fool they'll connect us. Good lord you're as big an idiot as the rest them."

Slamming the phone back in its cradle he stormed out of his office. As he opened the outer door the phone rang again.

"If whoever it is on the other end is in jail tell them they can stay there," he yelled at the two men in the outer office. "I'm not bailing out any more of you idiots this week. I'm done you hear me, done."

He was still ranting as he walked down the hallway and started down the stairs leading to the nightclub.

"Joey," one of the men called to him. "Hey Joey, it's your wife. You want me to tell her you're done or do you want to talk to her?"

"Idiots," he muttered as he headed back to his office. "I'm surrounded by damned idiots."

"Yeah," he said into the phone.

It wasn't his wife, it was Riley again.

"I thought I already took care of you," he said as he scowled at the two men with him.

"You still want her dead?" Riley asked him.

"I'm listening," he returned.

Riley told him what he had in mind.

"You do that," he said before he hung up, "and I'll see to it that you get out of town for good."

"Wearing cement shoes," he added after he hung up. "That will take care of that loose end once and for all."

The Doctor had given Carolyn a sedative in the Ambulance and she'd been asleep since. Karen stood by the hospital bed and looked down at her barely recognizable friend. Reaching out she stroked her hair before turning to leave.

"How could you," she said as she woke. "I trusted you."

"I didn't call Joey I promise," she apologized turning back around to face her. "Riley had been coming around threatening to close me down if I didn't tell him where you were. I got away with paying him off until you showed up on my doorstep. I don't know who tipped him off but he came by before Dawson showed up. I told him you weren't there, but he didn't care he wanted me to tell him where you were staying and that he'd wait for you. I didn't think you'd get hurt I swear."

She couldn't look at her anymore. She had a broken nose; her face was all swollen and turning black and blue. With three broken ribs, a collar bone, and a wrist she really wasn't able to turn away. Instead she closed her eyes telling her to go away.

With tears streaming down her face she left her friend's hospital room. She didn't see Abrams, or the three plain clothed detectives behind him, as they went into the room behind her.

He introduced the female officer as Gretchen Baldwin telling her that she would be sitting in her room at all times. He also told her that Dawson was the one that had suggested the officer.

"There'll be another one outside in the hallway," he told her. "So there shouldn't be any problems or unwanted visitors."

He bid her good night and left the officer behind.

Karen had made her way to Benson's room to collect Debbie Jo and to take her back home. However, she wasn't having any part of it.

"I promised I wouldn't leave him," she whispered holding his hand as he slept.

"Do you really think that a cop is going to want you around?"

"Why wouldn't he, there's nothing wrong with me."

"Did you forget what you do for a living?"

"I'm through," she added quietly, "I'll be out of the house as soon as he gets out of the hospital."

"Do you intend on staying here the whole time," she said starting to take out her anger with herself on the girl. "If you don't leave with me now you won't have a place to live."

"I got a place to go if I need it don't I Pop," she said as his father came into the room.

William 'Bill' Benson smiled at the girl as he limped into the room.

"Of course you do," he said making his way to the chair by the window. "If my boy wants you around then you'll always have a home with us."

"And before you say it," she added. "He knows what I am too."

"When his mother finds out what you are I don't want you to come crawling back to me," she said storming out of the room.

Debbie Jo looked at his father with tears forming in her eyes.

"Don't worry," he said. "It's just the two of us in the house. It'll be nice to have a woman around again. With any luck a few grandchildren too?"

Nodding she smiled and ran over to him wrapping her arms around his neck.

"Looks like you have a way with these Benson men," Abrams laughed as he came into the room.

She blushed, letting go of him she immediately went back to Carl and took a hold of his hand.

"Bill Benson," he said extending his hand as he recognized

the man in the chair. "I should have put the two names together."

"Seems to me you always did need a little help putting the easy stuff together," he laughed shaking the outstretched hand.

"Enough about me," he said shaking his head hoping to change the subject. "How's the leg?"

"I'll always have a limp but at least I'm still breathing," he said tapping his leg.

"They retired you didn't they?"

"It's not as bad as you'd think," he nodded. "No one's shooting at you and you don't have to go out in the rain or snow unless you want to."

"I might have to look into that."

"Who are you kidding?" he told him. "They'll have to push you out kicking and screaming, or end up like me, or worse."

He smiled nodding knowing that he was right. He then told him that he was leaving a detective there with them.

"Just on the off chance that they decide to come back and finish the job," he added.

"I don't think that's going to be a problem," he returned opening his jacket to show him what he had at his waist.

"He wake up yet?" he asked as he looked at the butt end of the thirty-eight that stuck out of the holster.

They both told him no.

"They took three slugs out of him," Debbie Jo added. "I don't think he'll wake up much before morning

"Feel like a little coffee?" he asked Bill.

"I could use another," he said standing up.

"Good let's go see if we can shake some up and you can tell me what you do with your time now."

Stepping off the elevator Karen walked into Dawson as he stood swaying slightly waiting to get on it. Her head bounced on his chest and she had to grab on to him to keep from falling.

"Most fun I've had waiting for the elevator in a long time," he joked looking down into her tear stained eyes. "Here now she isn't going to die on us is she?"

Using his thumbs he wiped away her tears. She managed a barely audible no before burying her face in his chest. As they stood there they were approached by a nurse who told them told they would have to leave. Reaching into his overcoat he pulled a buzzer and flashed it at her. She threw her hands up in the air and walked away muttering about too many coppers being there to suit her. Dawson smiled as he steered the girl back onto the elevator taking her back up to Carolyn's room. He wasn't surprised to see that Abrams had already set some of his people in place, but he was surprised to see the female officer sitting in a chair next to the window.

"Look who I found," he said holding Karen by the arm.

"I don't want to see her," Carolyn said closing her eyes again. "I told her to go away once and I meant it."

"I promised Pop that I would keep you safe," he returned. "Now if I thought that what happened today was within her power to start or stop I wouldn't have brought her back here."

His words gave away the fact that he was a little tight.

"I am supposed to be making a phone call so I don't have a lot of time for foolishness."

"It's okay Dawson," Karen said. "I know it's my fault and I can't blame her if she doesn't want to see me anymore."

She shook loose of his grip and turned to walk out of the room.

"Wait," Carolyn called changing her mind. "Come and sit with me."

"Now that's better," he smiled and tipped his hat as he turned to leave the room.

"Thanks," they called to him as he left.

Making his way unsteadily to Benson's room he noticed the two detectives at their posts at either end of the hallway. He tipped his hat to one then the other almost falling as he spun on his heels to face the one behind him. It took him several steps to realize that he was walking in the wrong direction. Using his hand to direct himself he pointed to the left spinning around until he was facing in the right direction again. After a couple of wrong rooms he finally found the one that held the kid and his new girl. She was still holding his hand as she sat in a chair next to him. With her head resting on the bed she slept lightly. The kid raised his free hand placing his finger up to his lips. Dawson raised his hand and nodded his head walking closer. Shaking his free hand he asked him how he felt.

"Like I was run over by a motorcycle, a car, and a truck," he answered trying not to laugh.

"That about covers them all I guess," he said smiling. "Tell me something. Did you see Riley before you were shot?"

"I have been thinking about that since they brought me in," he started. "I didn't even have time to get my gun out when they came around the car. I remember seeing three of them, the one that shot me and I saw two others in the side mirror. Everything from there is a little sketchy. I heard two more shots, I tried to pull my gun but I was afraid they would come back and put a few more slugs in me. I laid on the horn hoping it would look as if I had hit it when I slumped over the wheel. I remember seeing the three going up the stairs as I pushed against the horn. I can't be sure how long it was before someone grabbed my shoulder pulling me away from it. I think I had my eyes open, but I can't be sure because it gets fuzzy about there from the pain."

"So it could have been one of the original three or a fourth."

"Yeah," he added looking at the still sleeping girl.

"You make sure you take good care of her in the future," he told him patting his leg.

He smiled but the look of worry showed through the smile.

"I wouldn't worry about her past kid," he said seeming to know what was on his mind. "There isn't a girl in the business that wouldn't give it all up for the right man, and you're hers."

"I was more wondering what my Pop would say."

"I wouldn't worry too much," he said heading for the door. "Your Pop isn't the one that's in love with her."

He smiled, running his hand through her hair as Dawson left.

The two detectives were standing at the nurse's desk talking to the floor nurse as he came out of the room.

"What's up boys?" he asked weaving as he approached them.

"Trouble at the jail," one of them said. "We're trying to find Abrams."

He asked them what the trouble was and they told him.

"There's been a jail break of sorts."

"What do you mean of sorts and who is it that's gotten loose?" he asked knowing exactly who they were going to say.

"We'd better wait for Abrams," the second detective said.

"You wait for him you might all be dead depending on who it was that gave your boys the slip."

He slipped his buzzer out of his pocket and slapped it down on the desk. The detectives glared at it and then at him.

"Dawson," the first detective began, "you know there are penalties for using that Marshals buzzer when you aren't one."

"Who told you I wasn't?"

The detectives stammered for a minute as he picked up his badge and stuffed it back in his coat pocket.

"I'll just have to guess then and you can tell me if I'm right," he said beginning again. "Riley is on the loose, and I can just about imagine that he's not alone."

They looked at him and shook their heads. He asked them who was with him, they told him.

"It's that guy from the house earlier," the first detective said. "Bascom, he's a three time loser so he doesn't have anything more to lose."

"Just the two of them?"

"As far as we know," the second detective answered. "Seems that Riley got them to let him out of his cell, he knocked the officer out took his keys and let Bascom out. He was still in uniform so it was easy for him to walk out taking Bascom with him."

Looking between the two detectives he told them what he wanted them to do.

"Don't worry about Abrams," he added when he'd finished.

"I'll deal with him if I have to. The important part is that we keep these two alive. One of them wants to start a new life and the other wants to end one by getting married."

"Are you sure they'll come tonight," the second detective asked.

"Ask yourself what you would do if you knew there were witnesses to your crimes sitting around and you just broke out of jail."

"Get out of town," he returned.

"Maybe," Dawson said nodding, "then again maybe not. I know I would want to tie up any loose ends before I left town. And the middle of the night is the perfect time to do it."

It was an hour later when two uniformed officers stopped at the nurse's station on the first floor to ask which floor the wounded officer was on. Without looking up the nurse willing gave out the information. As the elevator doors opened on the right floor they waved to the two detectives huddled together at one end of the corridor.

"You the two they sent to relieve us," one of the detectives said waving back.

The two uniformed officers looked at each other then smiled nodding their heads.

"Great," one of them added.

"Yeah my wife's about to kill me," said the other. "Just check with the nurse. She can tell you what rooms Benson and the girl are in."

They waved again as the two detectives turned and disappeared down a connecting corridor.

"Hi fellas," she said when they came to the desk. "You're the replacements eh. You boys wouldn't be single would you? It gets awfully lonely around here at night, if you know what I mean."

"Yeah sister," the first added looking the nurse up and down. "I know what you mean."

"Yeah," the other added. "We're both single. Why don't you tell us which room Benson and the Masters girl are in. Then you can go dig up one of your girlfriends for my partner."

A buzzer sounded for one of the rooms. Giving them the information they wanted she left the desk to answer it.

"I'll be back," she called over her shoulder, "and I'll bring a friend."

As she left them the two uniformed officers pulled thirty-two automatics out of their jacket pockets and tightened the muzzles on them.

"How do you like the swing on that dame?" Harry 'Skeez' Bascom asked as she walked away.

"Yeah, yeah whatever," Riley returned. "We don't have time for that remember we got a job to finish."

"That we do," he said moving toward Sally Masters' room.

"Too bad you won't be seeing that girl again," he added under his breath as Riley walked away from him.

Bascom was at the door to Benson's room in a second and slipped inside. He wasted little time in firing three shots at the body on the bed. Turning he slipped back out of the room. Riley had been just as quick and just as accurate in Sally's room. Meeting again in the corridor they began to make their way back to the elevator and out of the hospital.

Standing or rather swaying between them and the elevator was Dawson along with the Nurse who was actually Officer Gretchen Baldwin.

"Where you boys goin so fast?" she asked as they came past the nurse's station again. "I told you I was going to bring a friend."

"Hello again Riley," he said leveling a forty-five at each of them. "I can't forget you either Mr. Bascom. Or do you prefer Skeez? I like Skeez myself so I think that's what I'll use if you don't mind too much, not that I really care if you do."

Officer Baldwin moved behind the nurse's station pointing her police issue thirty-eight revolver at the two men. While the two detectives, who had been waiting, pointed theirs from around the corner at the end of the corridor.

"You'll go to the chair for killing a cop," Riley told him

lowering his rod.

"Maybe," he said, "but for a dirty one I just might get a medal."

Bascom it seemed didn't want to waste any time on talking, raising his heater higher he pulled the trigger. As his finger began to move Dawson pulled the trigger on one of his own automatics. Before Bascom's bullet slammed into the chest of the officer, Bascom had a hole where his right eye used to be. Riley hesitated a second longer with the detectives warning him not to do anything he would regret.

"At least we got them," he said smiling, pointing behind him as he lifted his thirty-two and pulled the trigger.

Dawson had seen it coming and didn't wait to see if the shot he'd let off hit anything before both of his automatics barked three times each. Each of the six bullets found their mark as Riley was thrown against the wall, his eyes wide from surprise.

"No you didn't," he said as the body that was Officer Jason Riley slid down the wall to the floor.

The real nurse and two doctors rushed to the downed officer's side.

"What the hell is going on here?" Abrams asked running down the corridor.

"Hello Chester," Dawson said leaning against the wall.

"You're not bleeding again are you?" he asked him.

"No, but she is," he said pointing his thumb over to the nurse and doctors.

"Riley?" he asked.

"And Bascom," he told him as he bent over and picked up his brass.

"I just got word they'd made a break for it. What about the kid and the girl?"

He told him that they were safe and gave him a quick rundown on what had happened and what they had done.

"She going to be alright?" he asked one of the doctors as they took Baldwin away.

"That vest you made her wear saved her life," he returned.

"The bullet got through, but it isn't very deep. She'll probably be out of here before breakfast."

"Good," he told them. "I would hate to be the one to have to tell her kid that she wasn't coming home."

"How'd you know she had a kid," one of the detectives asked.

"I need a drink," he said making his way to the elevator. "You don't need me do you? I'm supposed to be making a phone call back at Mike's Place. The girls probably think I left them with the check by now. Either that or that I ran off to join the circus. Is the circus in town? Do you think I would make a good clown? Or how about one of those trap, trep, trap, oh you know those guys that swing in the air."

"I'm not done with you yet," Abrams called after him. "Come back here."

"Oh," he said sticking his head out of the elevator. "I would have a long talk with that Sally dame or whatever she's calling herself today. I bet she's got some pretty good stuff on Tuna that she'll be willing to part with now."

As the elevator doors closed they could hear him singing, very off key.

"Oh, he flies through the air with the greatest of ease that daring young man on the…"

"Dawson!" Abrams yelled.

"I bet I'd make a good one of those, whatever they are!" he yelled back.

Thirty minutes later at one thirty in the morning he walked through the door of Mike's Place and ordered a drink from their waiter. He couldn't miss Tiny sitting at his table with Andrea. Jane was up on stage again singing one of her favorite songs. Tiny had his back to him and was showing Andrea the story he'd written. She saw him, but he put one finger to his lips to keep her from saying anything. When he reached the table he kicked the chair breaking one of its legs making it fall from under him. As he fell Dawson grabbed the back of his shirt collar and lifted him on to his feet. Before he knew what was happening he spun Tiny around and landed a fist to his nose. Dropping him as the punch landed, he ended up lying on the floor shaking his head wondering what had just happened.

"If I told you once I told you a hundred times," he said standing over him. "Don't ever use that name again."

The waiter handed him his drink. Telling him that he was sure that he was behind he ordered two more.

"Anything good in the paper?" he asked picking it and sitting down.

"Nothing that I find darling," Andrea smiled.

"Same old garbage from Washington I see, 'it's just around the corner,'" he added tossing the paper on the floor next to Tiny. "You know I keep wondering just what it is that's around the corner."

Two nights later Joey 'Tuna' Fisher, sitting at his desk in his office, answered a call from another of his inside men with the police force. His informant was telling him everything that he heard his former mistress Carolyn Walsh was telling detective Chester Abrams about him. After Riley and Bascom had failed to do what they'd set out to do Joey was happy to wait it out knowing that sooner or later she wouldn't have the police protection that she was currently enjoying. He had enough of his people watching her, keeping him up to date on where she was and what she was doing. He was a patient man after all, that is to a point. As he hung up the phone he knew that he'd have to kill her now. There was no way he was going let some round heeled dame get the best of him. She knew way too much and nothing could save her now. He'd tried to keep the girl in check when she was with him but she would never have any of it. Now she was a liability that he couldn't afford. He was still in love with her and it showed at times but even if she came back to him there was no way he could keep her around for long. It was raining again and he listened to it as it fell against the window. Pouring himself a drink he walked to the window and watched it as it fell. He liked the rain and the way it washed the streets clean of some of the garbage.

"If only it could wash it all away," he snarled taking a sip of his drink.

Opening the window he took a deep breath of the damp night air. The smell of it always reminded him of growing up close to the docks. He used to like to stand on the dock and smell the air that as it came in from the sea.

In the outer office two men sat quietly waiting for their boss. They were digging around for a pack of cards with their back to the door. Neither of them heard it open or the intruder, dressed in black and wearing a mask, as he stepped inside. Two quick bursts of his muzzled automatic sent the two tumbling over the table they were sitting at.

"What are you two idiots doing out there?" he asked turning at the sound from the outer office.

As he called out, his door was pushed opened. He stood helpless with a bottle in one hand and his drink in the other as the intruder entered.

"Who are you and what you doing here?" he asked stepping toward his desk.

"I wouldn't do that if I were you," he said pointing the muzzled automatic at him. "It doesn't matter who I am."

"In that case," he began, as he calculated the distance to his own gun in the desk. "At least let me ..."

He tossed his drink at him and dove for the desk. The automatic popped three times before his arm caught the edge of it and he hit the floor.

"Why," he managed as he landed half surprised he was still alive.

His breathing was hard as the intruder leaned over him lifted his mask to better examine his handy work.

"Let's just say that was for Carolyn," he smiled at the gangster. "And this, well this is for me."

Joey's eyes widened recognizing the intruder. The automatic popped again and Joey 'Tuna' Fisher breathed no more.

Picking up his brass he made his way out of the office, down the stairs, and out of the club.

Outside on the street the chauffer slid behind the wheel of the car and took off his hat.

"Where to next sir?" he asked as soon as he started the car.

"Home," the man said opening the window shade on the opposite side of the nightclub.

As the car pulled away an explosion ripped through the second floor offices of the Tropical Sun nightclub. The morning papers would blame the explosion on an old gas line that had once been used for light in the old building, but the chauffer and his two passengers would know better.

"You really need to buy better gas from now on," called the female voice from the back. "This cheap stuff sounds like it's ruining your engine."

"As you wish ma'am," he replied as a smile flashed across his face.

"That reminds me," his boss added, "did you ever thank Cook for your box?"